RADEK

Star-Crossed Alien Mail Order Brides

SUSAN HAYES

ABOUT THE BOOK

What do you do when your friend's planet runs out of women? Join them for takeout, of course.

Radek is a prince with a problem. He wants to see the galaxy, but an ancient law forbids any member of the Romaki Dragon Clans from ever leaving their planet. So, what's a Romaki Snow dragon to do? Defy the law, hop a ride with a friend, and head for the far side of the galaxy, that's what.

As the Pyrosians prepare to claim their mates, all Radek has to do is sit back, enjoy the party, and keep one little promise – no shifting into a dragon while he's visiting Earth. What could be simpler?

This book contains a sassy chef whose dreams just went up in flames, and a runaway prince who came to Earth looking for answers - and found his destiny instead.

SUSAN HAYES

Radek (Book #6 of the Star-crossed Alien Mail Order Brides Series)

First E-book Publication: October 2018

Cover Design: crocodesigns.com

Editor: Dayna Hart

Published by: Black Scroll Publications

ISBN: 978-1-988446-36-3

As always, this story is dedicated to my Mum and Dad, for their love and support of their sometimes-crazy daughter, and to Karen, for so many years of laughter and friendship.

CHAPTER ONE

PRINCE RADEK MAKYRN seethed with frustration, but he took care not to show it as he made his way through the crowd of revellers filling the palace's largest ballroom. His parents were hosting a party in honour of their off-world guests, none of whom were aware that while they were enjoying themselves, their hosts had decided not to proceed with the trade talks. The Pyrosians had come all this way for nothing – again.

It took him a painfully long time to reach the edge of the crowd. Too many beings wanted a moment of his time. Some merely wanted to say hello, others flirted shamelessly, and the rest tried to use him as a messenger, hoping he would convey their wishes for meetings or favours to his mother. He politely greeted everyone, declined all flirtations, and forgot each message the moment he moved on. Even if he was inclined to help some of them, it was a waste of time to try. During their last meeting, his mother had proven yet again that she wouldn't listen to a word he said.

He was almost free when Savta found him, stepping into his path and placing her hand on his arm. "Good eve, Highness. Your mother sent me to find you."

Radek looked pointedly at her hand. "Did she also grant you permission to be so familiar?"

Savta moved her hand immediately. "She did not, though I am aware she wishes us to become much more familiar with each other, and soon."

"Are you also aware that I have not agreed to my mother's request, nor do I intend to?"

Savta tossed her long, dark hair back with a practiced gesture and laughed, but beneath the light, airy sound was an undertone of ice. "Be smart, Highness. If you refuse, she'll make it a royal command. I *will* be your consort. I promise, if you accept this fact gracefully, I will make sure you are well satisfied."

She didn't say more, but the threat was crystal clear. If he fought this, she'd make him regret it. He managed a broad smile. "Haven't you heard, Savta? I'm the foolish one in the family. I spend my days lost in writings about the past and contribute nothing to the present. Worse, I argue with the priests, my siblings, and even my parents, whose word is law."

Her perfect features creased into a momentary frown. "You'd defy your mother's wishes?"

"She can order me to take you as my consort until I find my mate. She can even command me to move you into my rooms at the palace, but not even the ruler of my clan can control where I sleep, or with whom. You may sleep in my bed one day, but when that day comes, I will sleep somewhere else."

"So be it. This could have been a pleasant and profitable interlude for us both while the search for our mates continues. Instead, you have chosen to insult and demean me. I won't forget this." She flounced off, no doubt to inform his mother what he'd said.

It was a good bet that by morning he'd be enduring another lecture from his mother about duty and responsibility, then ordered to take that venomous *traxyn* as his consort. "I'm starting to think the Gods have it in for me," he muttered as he finally reached the outer doors, leaving the warmth and noise of the ballroom behind.

Out on the balcony, the night air was cold enough to turn his breath to vapour. It cut through his anger and frustration, helping him find a small measure of calm. It was just enough to stop him from giving in to his desire to launch himself into the air and shift to his dragon form and fly away. Not that there was anywhere he could go. He was too well known on his homeworld to stay hidden for long, and no member of his species was permitted to leave Romak.

Centuries ago, the Romaki had travelled the cosmos. They had colonized other worlds, trading with some species and warring with others. Then, the colonies had started failing, the survivors returning home defeated by weather, cataclysm, or war. More colony ships were sent out, only to vanish into the void. The priests claimed it was a sign of the Gods' displeasure, a warning that any Romaki who left the planet would invoke Solun and Daga's wrath.

He stepped to the balustrade and leaned out to look at the palace grounds stretched out below, then raised his eyes to the star-filled sky. He didn't believe the priests. Everything he'd studied made him suspect it wasn't the Gods who wanted to keep his race bound to one planet but the priests who claimed to speak for them.

The doors opened again, releasing a blast of noise and light that filled the balcony and momentarily dimmed the stars. So much for his moment of peace.

He turned, then relaxed as he saw who it was – Vadir Rahal, one of the visiting Pyrosians. "Evening, Vadir."

"Highness." The dark-haired male replied in perfect Romaki and joined him at the railing. Vadir ran a highly profitable trading empire that spanned the length and breadth of known space. He'd been to Romak enough times the two had become friends, a fact that had landed Radek in trouble with both the priests and his parents more than once. While he acted as the diplomatic envoy to all off-world visitors, his position, while needed, was not officially recognized.

The two of them stared out at the stars for a while in companionable silence, but then Vadir asked a question Radek didn't expect. "When are they going to tell us the trade talks have been suspended?"

Radek turned, not bothering to hide his surprise. "How did you know?"

"I have my ways."

"Apparently. And to answer your question, I believe the plan is to inform you and the rest of the delegation tomorrow morning. Did you get anything agreed to before they decided to end the talks?"

"Some. Mostly extending existing agreements." Vadir shrugged. "It's not what I hoped for."

"That seems to be a common sentiment around here today. The only ones who will be happy about this are the priests, may Solun freeze their balls off."

"Talk like that is going to get you yet another lecture from the priests."

"They'll have to wait in line. I argued with my mother tonight, trying to get her to see reason. We need more trade, not less. We're becoming a shadow of what we once were, afraid of anything different or new. It has to stop."

"Given that she cancelled the rest of the talks, I'm going to guess she didn't agree with you."

Radek smacked a hand down on the railing. "She did not. She thinks I need to stop studying the past and make more of an effort to represent the family in the present."

"She's finally decided to give you some responsibility, then?"

"Hardly," Radek scoffed. "She wants me to take a consort until such time as one of us finds our mate."

"Who?"

"Savta."

Vadir curled his lip with distaste. "My condolences. Is there any way you can avoid this arrangement without angering your parents even more? I can't see you being happy with someone with Savta's temperament."

Radek laughed. "Too late. Savta and I had words on my way out here. I told her it would take a royal command before I'd accept her as my consort. I have no doubt my mother has already heard about it."

"And while you wait for your punishment, you're sitting out here, contemplating the stars." Vadir looked up. "Do you ever wish you could go out there and see the galaxy for yourself?"

"Every day," he admitted.

"You know, my mate is from a planet on the far side of the galaxy. We're going to be heading there once we leave Romak."

Curious to see where Vadir was going with this, he played along. "Earth, right? I had the pleasure of speaking with Lisa earlier today. She's looking forward to returning home for a visit. It sounds like an interesting place."

"Did she happen to mention the fact her species have legends about a mythical scaled creature that breathed fire and flew?"

"Many species have myths about monsters and creatures that never existed." Radek was trying to play it cool, but his interest was piqued.

"Mhmm," Vadir drawled. "Any of them have a word in their language for dragon?"

"What? Really?"

Vadir nodded, his smile broadening. "Really. As far as I can tell, it appears the Pyrosians weren't the only aliens to spend some time on Earth."

"Do you have proof of this? If you did, it could change everything! The priests claim any Romaki who defies the Gods and leaves the planet is punished and stripped of their magic. If there were Romaki on Earth in their dragon form, it proves the priests are wrong."

"I don't have proof, no. That's back on Earth." He paused for half a heartbeat before adding. "If you came with us, you could find the proof you need yourself."

"Came with you to Earth? Leave Romak?" Radek was still trying to absorb Vadir's news. His brain wasn't ready to process an invitation to fulfill his greatest wish and visit another planet.

"That's exactly what I mean. Unless you'd rather stay here and take your chances with Savta?"

"By Solun's frosty beard, no. If I go with you, all I'm risking is the wrath of the Gods and the potential loss of my magic. That's preferable to staying here with my mother and Savta."

Vadir clapped a hand to his shoulder. "I thought so."

"You realize if my parents figure out where I am and who I am with, it's not going to go well for you or any future trade talks?" Vadir would have already done a careful study of the risks versus potential rewards before he decided to make the offer, but Radek still felt it needed to be said.

"True. But if you come back with verifiable evidence the priests are wrong, think of all the opportunities that open up." Vadir spread his hands wide. "Increased trade. Renewed travel. Shipbuilding."

"And since you'll be the first to know what I find, you'll have the advantage?"

"Exactly. I'm going to make a businessman out of you, yet, Highness."

"Good. If this doesn't work out the way you hope, I'll be asking you for a job."

Vadir nodded, his expression serious for once. "I've got your back, but I'm confident you're not going to need my help."

"You can't be sure."

"I am. I can't tell you why, though. Ask me about it when we're on our way home from Earth."

"Believe me, I will. Which brings me to my next question – how do you plan on getting me off the planet?"

"That's easy enough. Tonight, I'm going to take you and several other VIPs on a tour of my ship. When the group leaves, you'll stay behind. Once we get official word the talks are suspended, Lisa and I will express our displeasure, return to the ship within the hour, and depart with my usual dramatic flair. We'll be halfway across the galaxy before anyone knows you're gone."

Radek nodded. "That will work. I'll leave a message behind, something to lead everyone to believe I left to avoid Savta and my mother but will be back in a few days. I've done it before. If I leave a few items with you tonight, can you bring them aboard with your own things?"

"Of course."

"Then, that's the plan." Radek looked around the grounds of the palace one last time. He'd grown up here, exploring every inch of the grounds. He'd learned to shift his form out in the wide stretch of lawn, practiced controlling his magic by freezing the fountains, and created a small crater in a distant corner while he was still mastering takeoffs and landings. If Vadir was wrong, this might be the last time he looked out at this view. He fixed it in his memory, then turned his back on the garden and all the memories it held. "I better start packing."

"SHIT!" Piper slammed her cell phone down on the table harder than she intended. There was a crackling sound, and when she picked it up again, the screen had a spectacular web of cracks in the center. "Double shit. This day better not get any worse."

She could deal with a busted cell phone. She wasn't coping as well with the news she'd just lost a job she hadn't even started yet. The restaurant had burned down before it even opened. At least the owner had promised that once they got the insurance figured out they'd rebuild, and her job would be waiting for her. She'd find a way to get by until then, she always did.

"This is now officially a double shot of espresso kind of morning." She set the phone down, carefully this time, and went to the kitchen in search of caffeine. After that phone call, she might even break out the whipped cream and vanilla syrup.

The mug was almost empty by the time she started feeling better. She'd done some math, checked her bank balance, and sent out emails to a few contacts to let them know she was looking for employment, again. She'd also decided not to tell her sister about the fire until after they got to the stadium. Aria was going to meet her match from the Star-Crossed Dating Agency today, and she was already determined to turn down the match and retreat to her safe, lonely life as a single mom. If she found out Piper's dream job had literally gone up in smoke, she'd use it as an excuse to stay home. Piper was determined to get Aria to the Gathering at BC Place Stadium. Maybe if she met this guy in person, she'd change her mind about turning him down.

Piper had joined the same dating agency, but so far there was no match for her in their database. Unlike Ri, if she ever got matched, she'd be ready to take off for another planet in a heartbeat. It would be the adventure of a lifetime. She could already see herself opening a restaurant on Pyros, offering Earth-style meals to an entire planet full of eager customers. Not to mention the fact that being on the other side of the galaxy might just put enough distance between her and Ri to let her live her own life.

Their mother had died when she was still a teenager, and Aria had stepped into the role of mother-figure and guardian, while Piper had dealt with her grief by rebelling against anyone and anything she could think of. She'd outgrown that phase years ago, but not before it had set the template for their adult relationship. It didn't help that she'd moved back in after Aria had her baby. She adored Melody and was happy to help, but the second Piper moved home again, they'd fallen into old habits.

"And now I'm moping like a teenager. Next thing you know I'll be digging out my black lipstick and writing bad poetry." She drained her mug and headed for the bedroom. It was time to get ready for the Gathering. She'd already picked the perfect outfit, a cute blue and white mini-dress that happened to be a perfect match for her freshly dyed hair. She might not be one of the lucky matches, but she planned on looking good and enjoying herself anyway. If nothing else, five hundred hot aliens ready to meet their matches should make for a hell of a view.

SEVERAL HOURS LATER, she and her sister's best friend, Haley, had claimed their seats and spotted Aria among the women nervously waiting to meet their matches. The stadium roof was open, letting the summer sunshine pour in. The organizers had set up a beautiful open-sided white tent decorated with lavish displays of flowers. Aria was seated near the front, close enough to the edge that they could see her as she bounced Melody in her lap. The women were all seated beneath the tent, chattering to each other as they tried to subtly sneak looks at the stage and the men standing around it. Judging by their matching uniforms and serious expressions, they had to be the Pyrosians, but apart from their larger builds, they looked human enough.

Movement on the near side of the stage caught her attention. She watched with interest as two men, both wearing what had to be hand-tailored suits, appeared. They were followed by several more of the uniformed aliens, who seemed to be acting as bodyguards. They must be VIPs. They were both good-looking, one dark-haired, the other so blond his hair looked almost white. It was the blond who kept her attention. He kept looking around the stadium, his expression one of intense interest. A blonde woman in a bright orange and yellow sundress joined the men, and Piper exhaled in relief when she greeted the dark-haired one with a kiss, but only smiled at blondie. *Because it's totally rational to feel possessive about a total stranger.*

Once she got over her irrational response and focused on the woman, she realized she recognized her. "Is that one of the women from the Star-Crossed ads?" Piper asked Haley.

"I think so, yeah. So that guy she just smooched must be her mate."

Haley started snapping pictures with her phone. Later, Piper planned to ask her for some of them since she couldn't take any herself. Not with her phone in its current condition. More people started arriving, all of them smartly dressed and accompanied by a camera crew. They exchanged greetings and handshakes with the two men she'd been watching, and then all of them headed for their seats in a roped off area beside the stage.

Down on the stadium floor, the women waited for their matches with growing nervousness, and around the stage, there was a flurry of activity.

She didn't even notice the space shuttle descending into the arena until everyone around her started to gasp and point upward. At the same time, several columns of identically dressed men marched into sight. They were all staring at the women seated beneath the tent, and even from this distance, there was no mistaking their eager, hopeful expressions. One day, she wanted a guy to look at *her* that way.

With that wish still in her head, she looked away from the spectacle to scan the VIP seating. The handsome blond she'd been crushing on was watching the shuttle approach, but after a second, his gaze shifted, and she could almost swear he was looking back at her. Before she could be sure, though, the stadium erupted into a cacophony of flames, fire, and screams.

CHAPTER TWO

SINCE THE MOMENT Radek entered the stadium, something had been agitating his dragon. That part of his nature had been almost dormant since leaving home, and he was happy to have confirmation that, despite the priests' dire warnings, he hadn't lost access to his beast or his magic. Still, the creature's unease was making it difficult to focus. Worse, he couldn't tell what the problem was. Was it the planet's atmosphere? The lighter than normal gravity? The strangely delicious human food called poutine he'd eaten for lunch?

"Find. Take. Claim," his dragon hurled the words into his awareness but he had no idea what the beast was going on about. Yes, he was attending a claiming ceremony, but as a guest, not a participant.

"Find!" The last word came through as a roar that reverberated inside his skull so loudly he winced.

Lisa, Vadir's vivacious human mate, reached out to touch his arm. "You okay?" she asked in English.

"My uh…other half has his tail in a twist about something, and he's not being quiet about it," he whispered. The one thing they had all agreed on before arriving on this planet was that it would be best not to mention his abilities or the fact that his entire species were able to transform into a creature straight out of this planet's mythos.

"Any idea why?" she asked.

"None."

She nodded and hummed in sympathy. "I'm sure you--he? Will feel better soon."

He sure hoped so. It was going to be a long ceremony if he had to deal with his dragon's foul mood the entire time.

A few minutes later, the royal shuttle appeared overhead. He was watching with interest as it maneuvered through the relatively small opening in the roof, but something made him look at the mostly female crowd that had been invited to observe today's gathering. They had all joined the Star-Crossed Dating Agency in hopes of meeting their mates, and they had been offered tickets, so they could see firsthand what they could look forward to one day.

He didn't know what he was looking for until he spotted a stunning female with bright blue hair. She met his gaze, and his dragon roared a single word. *"Claim!"*

Not possible. He was on his feet even as he denied what his dragon was telling him. Then the first explosion hit.

He acted out of instinct, summoning his magic and

forming a shield of pure energy around himself and the other guests. Chunks of debris slammed into the barrier and bounced away again, but not even his magic could block the ear-pounding detonations and the wails of fear that erupted all around him.

Vadir leaped up, grabbing his mate's hand and drawing her in tight to his side. "How long can you hold this?" he shouted the question to be heard over the din.

"Long enough to get us out of here. Make for that door." Radek gestured to a large opening behind them. "Go!"

Vadir and Lisa dashed for the doorway with many of the other guests following them out of blind panic. Radek stood his ground, impervious to the destruction going on around him. By the time Vadir noticed he wasn't with them, it was too late for him to do anything about it but shout, "Get out of there!"

Radek shook his head and gestured for the two of them to get to safety. Once his friends were through the door, he dispelled the shield and turned back towards the last place he'd seen the blue-haired woman. The one his dragon was insisting was his mate.

"*Find. Protect!*" The beast was in a frenzy, testing the limits of his control as he moved through the chaos and carnage. Smoke and dust filled the air, limiting visibility. He drew in a deep breath, ignoring the acrid smoke and the more disturbing odour of death as he channelled the powers of his dragon to track his mate's scent. He might not be ready to accept it, but his dragon was convinced the female was theirs.

He breathed in again, and this time he caught a trace of something. *Her.* Her scent. Her…blood? No! He ran towards the scent, charging straight through an explosion that left his human-style clothing shredded and charred. The seating area where he'd last seen her was empty, but her scent was stronger the closer he got. She couldn't have made it far.

The stairs were strewn with rubble, so instead of slowing down to navigate the uneven terrain he leapt over it and kept going as yet another explosion rocked the floor beneath his feet. There was another pile of still-smoking debris twenty meters up. He made straight for it, ignoring the icy knot of dread forming in his stomach. He found her pinned beneath a large chunk of concrete, one hand flung out as if she were reaching for someone behind her. Her face was pale beneath the streaks of blood and dust, her eyes were closed, and there was a trickle of blood flowing out from under the stone pinning her, dripping down the stairs to form a crimson pool.

"Protect!" The dragon roared in his head. Before he could react, the creature took over, lifting the debris and casting it aside. It landed in an empty stretch of chairs, crushing them flat. The concrete had done much the same thing to his female's legs. Radek was grateful she was unconscious, so she didn't have to endure the agony such an injury would inflict.

He dropped to his knees at her side, fighting the

dragon for control. He had to know if she was alive, or if the Gods had decided to punish him for leaving home by offering him his mate, only to take her life before they could be together. He touched her lips, sighing in relief when her breath warmed his finger. She was alive, for now. He looked down at her damaged body and the growing pool of blood. If he didn't do something, she wouldn't stay that way for long.

His dragon uttered a single word. *"Claim."*

"We can't. She hasn't given her consent." But as he looked at her, Radek knew the beast was right. It was her only chance. It would take too long to get her back to the *Firebrand*, even in dragon form. He didn't know if what he planned would even work, but he had to try.

"Ours to protect." His dragon insisted.

He leaned down and brushed a gentle kiss to his mate's lips. "Forgive me for doing this without your permission, *sadina*." He bowed his head until his mouth grazed the side of her neck. He opened himself to the beast inside him, and they claimed her together, his fangs sinking into her throat. His magic flowed into her, binding their souls together.

It was done quickly, and he gathered her into his arms, ignoring the blood and gore that soaked into his already ruined clothes as he cradled her close to his chest, He needed to get her away from here, far from danger and out of sight. If she woke again, they'd both be consumed by the *rux*, the mating fever that accompanied the claiming. And if she didn't wake it would be safer for the inhabitants of this world if he, and his dragon, were somewhere isolated while they dealt with their grief.

"She will wake." His dragon was far more certain then he was. He knew that in the past, some members of other races had taken Romaki mates. After the mating, they had become dragons, but there was no way to know if it would work with a human. Even if it did, her injuries were severe. It might not be enough to save her life.

As the thought of losing her loomed in his mind, it happened.

She gasped, then sagged as she exhaled for the last time. He waited, watching and praying for her to take another breath. Time slowed, then stopped. Grief filled him, as cold and barren as the highest peaks of his homeland. She was gone.

Bereft and broken, he bowed his head to whisper a prayer for the swift passing of her soul. The moment his lips touched her forehead a surge of power slammed into him, stronger than anything he'd ever experienced. He was dazed for a moment, and when his senses returned it was to the most incredible sight of his life. His mate was looking up at him with eyes the colour of a summer sky. She lived. The conversion had worked.

Elated, he rose to his feet with her still in his arms. As he stood, he whispered the words of a sleeping spell that would keep her safe and unaware until he could bring her somewhere isolated, so they could talk.

Once she was asleep, he transformed, giving himself over to his dragon despite his promise not to alter form while on Earth. Vadir and the Pyrosian prince would have to forgive him, but the needs of his mate came first.

He kept hold of her while he shifted, then cradled her carefully in his talons as he stretched his wings and took to the air with a roar that echoed across the stadium.

After weeks of being confined to his bipedal form, it felt incredible to fly again. He rose quickly, eager to get away from the chaos. Once he cleared the stadium, the air cleared quickly, but he continued to climb. The higher he went, the less likely it was he'd be spotted. The shuttlecraft carrying the prince and his party were barely discernable in the sky above him. They'd be safe aboard the *Firebrand* soon. Hopefully, Vadir and Lisa weren't far behind. He briefly considered returning to the ship, too but rejected the idea almost immediately. While the Pyrosian's flagship was certainly safe, it hadn't been designed with the needs of dragons in mind. Over the next few days, he and his new mate would require space, privacy, and possibly room to fly.

He dipped one wing and changed course, making straight for the mountain range beyond the city. There had to be a spot within all those wild, unpopulated acres where he and his mate could stay out of sight until the *rux* passed. He was already envisioning the bower he would make for them, filled with every delight and luxury he could think of. He'd need to consult his mate about meals, of course. His magic allowed him to create whatever foods they'd need, but he would have to consider her preferences. Would she prefer sweets or savoury dishes? Spicy or simple? He had so many questions to ask her, and no doubt, she would have even more questions for him.

Still, the Gods had given him this female to cherish and protect. She was living proof that the future of his race was out among the stars, not hiding away on Romak. The Gods wouldn't have chosen her if she wasn't strong enough to accept her new life, and him.

PIPER WAS HAVING the most amazing dream. First, she'd been flying over the city, watching the buildings and cars pass beneath her as if they were perfectly crafted miniatures. Then she'd left the city behind and flown into the mountains, soaring over forests and peaks that she'd only ever seen from the ground. Eventually, she started to descend, which was weird, considering she hadn't wanted the flight to end. A clearing opened up below and she circled around it, spiralling in for a landing among the grass and wildflowers that covered the space.

Like dreams often do, this one skipped a bit, and she found herself stretched out among the flowers, staring up at the sky. *Boring. I liked flying better.* Things got a lot less boring when she heard someone talking in a strange, sing-song way. A male someone. She lifted her head. The blond hottie from the Gathering was standing a few feet away. He was facing her, but his eyes were focused on something in the distance. The best part about her dream was that he wasn't wearing anything but a smile wide enough she saw his fangs... Wait. Fangs? Since when did her sexual fantasies include vampires? For that matter, why was she dreaming at all? She was supposed to be at the Gathering with Aria, wasn't she?

She pinched her arm, but nothing happened. She was still lying in a field with a hot, naked blond guy. Alarmed, she sat up so fast her head spun, but that didn't stop her from noticing her clothes were a bloodstained mess. *What the hell is going on?* She started going over herself with trembling hands, trying to find the source of the blood. Why didn't she feel any pain? Oh God, was she paralyzed?

"You won't find any injuries. You are healthy and quite perfect."

She looked up with a start. Blondie was standing right beside her now, his white-blond hair gleaming in the summer sun as he looked down at her with grey eyes. No, not grey, silver. Weirder still, he was suddenly dressed in a blue, toga-like garment that left his arms and lower legs bare and did amazing things for his shoulders.

"You were at the Gathering. You're Pyrosian, right? I was there, and now I'm... here." She gestured wildly to indicate the clearing. "Where is here? And who are you, and what happened back at the stadium? I remember explosions and screaming and...oh god. Haley. Aria. Melody!"

He dropped to his knees at her side and wrapped a strong arm around her shoulders. "I am Radek Makyrn, and yes, I was at the Gathering, but I am not Pyrosian. I will explain matters once we're inside."

"Hey, hands off!" She shoved his arm away. "And inside where? We're in the middle of a freaking forest!"

Radek stayed where he was. Only his arm moved as he pointed to something behind her. "Inside there."

"If I look, are you going to try and touch me again?"

He shook his head. "I will stay where I am, *sadina*. You have my word."

"Fat lot of good that does me," she muttered. "I don't know you, so I have no idea if you're the kind of man who keeps his word or not."

His shoulders stiffened, and his dazzling eyes darkened several shades at her words. "I am Prince Radek of the planet Romak, my mother rules the Snow Dragon Clan of my homeworld, and I swear on her life and those of my family that I will not touch you again without your consent."

"Uh huh. Sure. I'm totally willing to believe I've been abducted by an alien dragon prince. That might explain the fangs, but I'm still not buying it. When I turn around, am I going to see your spaceship?" She turned and looked behind her, expecting to see nothing but trees. Instead, she saw a gleaming building with a vaulted roof and walls that looked like they were made of solid crystal. The structure was only two stories tall, but its footprint took up a good portion of the clearing. "That's not a spaceship."

"It is not. Even if I possessed such a thing, it wouldn't be as comfortable as the home I have made for us."

She looked back to see he had kept his word and stayed still. "You made that? Out of what? It looks like crystal, or maybe snow? But it can't be. It's the middle of summer."

He offered her his hand. "I mentioned I am a snow dragon, did I not? Come, see for yourself." He paused, then added. "And will you please tell me your name?"

She looked at him and then the ice house and back to him again. Nothing made sense at the moment, which left her with a choice. She could either freak out, run into the woods and probably get lost then attacked by some rabid woodland creature, or she could give in and embrace the madness. It wasn't a difficult choice. She leaned forward and took his hand, doing her best to ignore the fact even that simple contact made her breath catch in her throat. "I'm Piper."

His smile widened as he got to his feet without letting go of her hand. "I'm happy to meet you, Piper." The moment he was standing, he helped her up and then shifted his grip so he could continue to hold her hand.

When she looked down at their hands, he uttered a low, sensual chuckle that made her tingle in some interesting places. "I said I wouldn't touch you without your consent. You indicated I could hold your hand, so I intend to keep doing so."

"My sister warned me about guys like you."

"I doubt that. There's no one else like me around for lightyears."

That charming smile returned, and her heart did a double-beat, followed by a backflip. Before she knew it, she was moving closer, until they were almost touching. "I don't understand any of this. Not you, or how we got here, or why…" she trailed off as she raised a hand, stopping just before her fingers reached his cheek.

"Do you wish to touch me?" he asked.

She blushed and nodded once, feeling foolish. She didn't know him at all, but her body didn't care. She wanted to connect with him. God, she wanted to do so much more than connect. She wanted to climb him and rub herself all over him like she was a cat and he was catnip.

"What you're feeling is called the *rux*. I feel it, too," he ran his thumb across the back of her hand. "You may touch me, *sadina*. I would welcome it."

She caressed his cheek for a brief moment but withdrew before she was tempted to do more. "Why is it every time you tell me something, it leads to more questions?"

"Because you are as bright as you are beautiful, Piper of Earth. Now, will you come with me? There are things I need to tell you, and questions you need answered."

"Is one of those things going to be how you managed to be naked one second and dressed the next?" she asked as he led her toward the structure he claimed to have created. She still wasn't ready to believe him about that.

"You saw that?" he asked.

"Uh huh. Skyclad is a good look for you."

"I'm not familiar with that term. It wasn't part of my language upload."

"It means wearing nothing but air. Bare-assed naked." She almost commented that it was a very fine ass, too. "Now, will you please tell me what happened at the Gathering?" It was only a short walk to the strange building, and the closer she got, the more out of place it looked. She'd thought maybe it was a tourist attraction or an art installation, but now she could see it was exactly what he said it was. A house carved from ice in the middle of nowhere, at the height of summer.

Radek continued talking as they walked toward the impossible structure. "There was an attack. Multiple explosions detonated in a short period of time. I saw my friends to safety, then went looking for you."

"Why would you go looking for me? We're strangers."

They reached the door, and he pushed it open, giving her only a moment to admire the elaborately detailed dragon carved into the center of it. "I went after you, Piper of Earth, because I had to. You are my *sadina*, my chosen mate."

CHAPTER THREE

"I'M YOUR WHAT?" she demanded, stopping dead in her tracks.

"Mate. The one chosen by the Gods to stand at my side for the rest of our lives. In my language, you are my *sadina*."

Folding her arms across her chest she shot back, "I have a word for you in my language, too: bonkers."

He cocked his head and looked at her like a confused but adorable puppy. "What does that mean?"

"It means I think you're crazy. If we were mates, I'd know it, wouldn't I? There'd be a spark or something, right?"

"I'm a Romaki Snow Dragon, not a Pyrosian. We don't do fire or sparks, and I am not mentally unbalanced!" He sounded so indignant she almost giggled.

"Fine. You're a Romaki." She couldn't bring herself to say the word dragon. It was just too much weirdness, even for her. "What the hell makes you think I'm your mate? Is it the hair? I hate to break it to you, but it's dyed. I'm really a brunette."

"It is not your hair, or your beauty, or your temper. All of those things make you attractive to me, but it's not why I know you are mine." He touched his chest. "My soul recognized yours the moment I entered the stadium today. My dragon understood it before I did because I never imagined I would find you here, so far from home."

"And does this dragon speak to you a lot?" She was starting to wonder if her sexy alien saviour really was mentally unbalanced.

He grinned. "At times. He is part of me, but not all of me, if that makes sense. He is my wild side and the source of my magic."

She held up her hand. "I've got information overload. Let's set aside the whole 'my magic dragon talks to me' thing for now and get back to my earlier question. You seem convinced I'm your mate. If that's so, shouldn't I know it, too?"

"Your soul knows it is so. That's what the *rux* is." He moved to face her, then gestured between them. "What we're feeling is the physical confirmation of our destiny."

"Lust isn't destiny." She'd been slow to learn that lesson, but after repeated heartbreak, she'd figured it out.

"This is not lust." He held his hand out. It was shaking slightly. "I crave your touch. I need to know what you taste like, how your hair will feel when I run my hands through it. This is the *rux*, and soon it will consume us both."

A rush of raw need flooded her senses, accompanied by the thought that it had been a long time since she'd been *consumed*, which was completely beside the point right now. She fought down a sudden urge to step into his arms and kiss him until they were both breathless, took a deep breath and said, "You're gorgeous and all, but I'm pretty sure I can resist the urge to jump into bed with you until we know each other better. Hell, you haven't even told me how I got here or why my clothes are torn and bloody."

"You were injured when I found you. A large chunk of concrete had crushed your legs and you were unconscious." His voice lowered as he described how he'd found her and there was a note of pain in his tone. "I did what I had to do. I healed you, then shifted forms and flew you somewhere we wouldn't be disturbed."

Her head spun. "You flew me here? How? And how did you heal me? And for that matter, if you can heal, why didn't you stay and help? My sister and her baby were there waiting for her match, and I was sitting with a friend! Why did you abandon everyone else?"

He frowned. "I did not abandon anyone. There is nothing I could have done to heal anyone but you. If you weren't my mate, it wouldn't have worked. If I hadn't been there today, you would have died. In fact, I think you did die for a moment. You stopped breathing for so long I thought I'd lost you."

"I stopped breathing?"

"You did. Long enough for me to believe I'd finally found my mate only to lose you before we even got to speak."

She believed him. It didn't seem possible, but either he was the best actor in the galaxy, or he truly thought she had died. "And you couldn't have saved anyone else? Just me?"

"Only you," he confirmed. "I am sorry about your family and friend. I'm sure you are worried about them. If it's any help, I didn't see any explosions go off near the human females waiting for their matches. Whoever did this set most of the explosive devices where they would harm the Pyrosians, not humans."

She glanced down at her ruined clothes. "Most, but not all. And if I was hit, then Haley must have been too." A fragment of memory flitted through her mind, and she stopped talking to try and bring it into focus. They'd been running up the stairs. Haley was finally moving faster now she'd kicked off her shoes. They were almost to an exit level. She'd turned around to check on Haley and then – nothing. "I don't remember what happened to her. You need to take me back. They might be hurt!"

He shook his head. "I can't do that."

"Of course you can. You got us here, you can take me back." Even as she said it, part of her protested the idea of leaving. She needed to stay here with Radek, didn't she?

"It wouldn't be safe. I told you my dragon represents the wild, more primal side of my nature. What do you think will happen if I fly you back into the city while we are affected by the *rux*? Do you see that ending well for anyone?"

He really seemed convinced he was a damned dragon. She wanted to keep dismissing the idea, but that was getting difficult to do, considering she was standing in a building carved from ice in the middle of a forest, covered in blood but without a scratch on her. "Look, I'm having trouble with this whole dragon thing. Can you prove it to me? I think I'm going to need to see it to believe it."

He gestured around them. "Not in here. I just built this, I'd rather not flatten it before you even look around."

"You're that big?" She knew she'd made a mistake the second the words left her lips.

He gave her an arrogant, toe-curlingly sexy smile. "You've seen me, what was the word, skyclad? You know the answer to that already, *sadina*."

Oh god. She did, and now her brain was happily replaying that memory on a loop, which was making it hard to think about anything else. "Outside. You go outside and tell me when you're ready for your big reveal. No! I mean call me when you're ready to show me your dragon. I mean… dammit, you know what I mean. I'll look around the house that magic built. Call me when you've unleashed the beast."

He was laughing as he bowed to her. "As my mate wishes. I will call you when I'm ready."

She uttered a frustrated squawk and waved him off, then started fanning her overheated cheeks. "I cannot believe I said those things. What the hell is wrong with me?"

"The *rux* is taking hold. We don't have much time left," he replied from somewhere outside.

"Hot, smart, charming, and he's got the hearing of a bionic bat. Great."

Gifted with a few minutes of solitude, she tried to distract her whirling mind by looking around while finger-combing out the worst of the knots in her hair. The first thing she did was walk over to one of the walls and press her hand to it. It looked and felt like a solid block of ice. It was translucent, cool, and slippery smooth, but the air around it wasn't chilled at all. Her fascination grew as she turned to explore. The roof was vaulted, and the inside was decorated with carvings, mostly decorative, swirling patterns, but she saw the same dragon motif she'd seen on the door repeated in a few other places.

The living space was a wide-open design with a fireplace as the focal point. Sure, the flames were blue, it gave off little heat, and there was no fuel source she could see, but it was still some kind of fire. "He'll probably tell me it's magical, too," she muttered as she continued looking around. The furniture appeared to be made of the same stuff as the walls. Simple, almost blocky, designs covered in thick, sumptuous fabrics and cushions in various shades of silver, blue, and white. There was a lounge and chairs near the fire, and beyond that was a massive bed piled high with blankets and pillows.

One look at the bed and her imagination went into overdrive. If she stayed, this is where they'd sleep. Both of them, together. *Skin to skin. Limbs tangled, asleep in each other's arms...* God, she wanted that so badly she could taste it. She held out her hand and discovered it was shaking just like Radek's had. She spun around and started for the door before she even knew what she was doing.

"Need," the word was barely a whisper in the back of her mind, and it accompanied another wild surge of lust.

"Yeah, I *need* to get a grip."

She hadn't reached the door when there was an earth-rumbling roar from outside. Either there was a mutant bear out there, or Radek wasn't crazy after all.

She ran the last few steps and burst through the door, then stopped dead as she spotted a massive, blue and silver creature standing in the middle of the clearing. "Holy shit!"

Radek was huge, and he was most definitely a dragon, wings, tail, teeth, and all. He was covered in iridescent blue scales that shimmered in the sunlight. The only part of him that hadn't changed were his eyes, still the same familiar silver. With a low rumble that sounded suspiciously like laughter, he sat up straighter and spread his wings, showing off for her.

Speechless, Piper could only stare in wonder. He was breathtaking. No picture or statue could compare to the creature before her. Only, he wasn't a creature. This was Radek. Which meant it was all real. Magic. Dragons. Shapeshifters. She'd fallen into a fairy tale.

She raised a hand and took a step towards him, then stopped. Common sense dictated you didn't just walk up to a dragon and pet it like a puppy, but her fingers itched with the need to touch him.

Another step. "It's still you, right? You're okay with me touching you when you're like, uh, this?"

In response, Radek furled his wings and carefully lowered himself to the ground. Once he was settled, he let his head drop onto the grass a few feet in front of her and gave a brief rumble.

"I'm taking that as a yes." She walked up to the side of his head and gently placed her hand on him. She expected the scales to feel cold and hard and was surprised when the warm, smooth surface gave slightly under her fingers. "So, I guess I owe you an apology for calling you bonkers, earlier. But can you blame me? Dragons are supposed to be mythical. How was I supposed to know they were actually aliens from another planet?"

He uttered another low rumble, and this time she was certain it was laughter. "Quit that. It isn't nice to laugh at your mate on your first date."

Two seconds later she wasn't petting a dragon

anymore. Instead, she was looking down at a very naked Radek lying on the grass at her feet.

"Say that again," he demanded as he bounced to his feet.

"You forgot your clothes," she pointed out as she fought, and failed, to stop staring at him. He was a gorgeous dragon, but dear god, he was panty-melting sexy as a man. Broad shoulders that tapered down to a trim waist and six-pack abs the likes of which she'd only seen on the cover of romance novels and fitness magazines. Her gaze drifted lower, and she had to bite her lip to stop herself from moaning aloud as she got a good look at his cock. He was hung like a…well, like a dragon, and there were subtle ridges down the length of his shaft that almost made her laugh out loud as the words 'ribbed for her pleasure,' sprang to mind.

He walked right up to her, then swept her into his arms, pressing her against his hard, naked body. "Say it again, Piper."

"Say what?" she asked. She'd never been this turned on in her life, and it was making it impossible to think of anything but what she wanted to do to him, and what she needed him to do to her.

"You called yourself my mate." He cupped her chin in his hand and lifted her head, to stare into her eyes. "Tell me who you belong to, *sadina*, and I'll give you what you need."

One look in his silver eyes and she knew the truth, even if she didn't understand how it was possible. A wave of lust slammed into her, so powerful it made her sway in his arms. "I belong to you, Radek. And you belong to me."

RADEK WANTED to throw back his head and roar in triumph. She had consented. More than that, she had claimed him as her own. He bowed his head and slanted a hard kiss across her mouth. He'd been waiting for this moment since she had first woken, and her response was all he could have hoped for. She rose on her toes to kiss him back, her arms twining around his neck as she parted her lips and let him taste her properly.

As tempted as he was to lay her down and take her right here in the meadow, he was determined to do better. "Hold onto me."

She moved back enough to grin at him. "I thought I was already doing that."

"You are intoxicating," he said as he cupped his hands under her ass and lifted her into the air.

"And you're a dragon." She was giggling as she wrapped her legs around his hips. "Why do I feel like I'm drunk?"

"In a way, you are." He stopped to kiss her again, letting his tongue savour the depths of her mouth. She tasted sweeter than sun-ripened *veli* berries, his favourite dessert. His curiosity was piqued when he discovered her tongue was pierced. He'd read about this practice in his research about humans, along with numerous references to its benefits. His mate was full of surprises.

Kissing Piper was a delectable torment. He wanted to continue, but he needed to do more than kiss her, he needed to explore every inch of her body and learn all the ways he could give her pleasure. Finally, he tore his mouth from hers and started back toward the home he had conjured for them.

"The *rux* is doing this? You Romaki don't mess around with your mating rituals, do you? I can't keep a thought in my head. I know I should be worried about my family, but I'm not. It's like I'm not in control of my brain right now. I don't like it."

"This feeling will pass, but not quickly." He did a quick bit of math. "It will be at its peak for three or four of your planetary rotations, though the effects will take much longer to fade completely."

"That long? Everyone is going to be worried about me."

He knew how she felt. No one knew where he was, and he had no way to let them know. His communicator hadn't survived the explosion that had destroyed his clothes, and he was too deep into the *rux* to leave Piper for more than a few minutes. His friends would be worried, but there was nothing he could do, and it was safer for everyone if they weren't found until the mating fever passed. He hadn't even told Piper the truth about how he'd healed her, yet. She wasn't likely to react well to the news that to save her life, he'd had to turn her into a dragon. "I have no way to contact anyone, or I would have already done so."

Piper buried her face in the crook of his neck and sighed, her breath a warm caress against his bare skin. "You can conjure a fully furnished house from thin air, complete with freaky ice that doesn't melt and blue fire, but you can't send a simple message? No walkie-talkie spells in your repertoire? Oh, could you summon a messenger owl? That would be cute."

"I can't summon living things or send messages, no. My species believe that the Gods put limits on our magic to ensure we didn't try to take their place one day."

She nipped his neck, and that brief sting made his cock harder than stone. "Your species think pretty highly of yourselves, huh?"

"I'll tell you all about it later. Right now, I have other plans for us." He pulled her in tight, rubbing his hard length against her body to make his point.

"Promise me that the moment we can, we'll find a way to make contact. I need to know the people I love are safe."

"I promise."

She lifted her head and gave him a look so full of hunger it made his blood boil and his heart race. "Then there's nothing left to say, is there?"

"Only this. You are mine, Piper. And no matter what comes, there isn't a force in the universe that will stop me from protecting what is mine."

He carried her back inside, kicking the door shut

behind him. He knew where he wanted her, and what he wanted to do once he got her there. Walking past the bed, he stepped into the bathing chamber he'd envisioned and looked around in approval. There was a sink with several pitchers of water for washing, and a polished portion of the wall that served as a mirror. He could create water in abundance, as well as enough basic foodstuffs to keep them well supplied for the next few days.

It was traditional for a newly mated male to create a place like this for his mate and fill it with every comfort he could conjure. For the next few days, he intended to pamper his *sadina*. She was the gift of a lifetime, not only for himself but for the future of his species.

CHAPTER FOUR

Piper looked around with interest. She hadn't made it this far in her brief exploration. "We have running water?"

"Of a sort." He glanced up to the ceiling. "There's a cistern on the roof full of water. Just don't hop into the shower without telling me, first. I'll need to heat it."

She laughed. "I'll try to remember that. Though given the way I'm feeling, an ice-cold shower might help."

He set her back on her feet and cradled her face in his hands. The expression on his face was fierce and tender at the same time, and it made her feel like she was the most important thing in his world. "Cold water wouldn't keep the *rux* at bay for more than a few minutes. I know this is sudden, and you still have questions. I swear by the love Solun holds for his lady you will be alright, and once this passes we will find your family."

"So, you're saying trust the hot alien dragon guy, and all will be well?" It was insane, but she did trust him. It didn't make any sense, but she did.

He stroked his thumb across the kiss-swollen curve of her mouth. "Yes, my beautiful human mate, that's what I'm saying. You can trust me. I would die before I allowed any harm to come to you."

She moved into his embrace, placed her hands on his bare chest, and rose up on her toes to kiss him. There wasn't any need for words anymore.

His answering kiss was so heated it stole her breath away. He covered her mouth with his, sealing in her soft moans of need. Their tongues tangled, and she quickly learned to be aware of the sharp points of his fangs. She'd never been much for biting, but the idea of him using those fangs on her sent a fresh jolt of desire sizzling through her veins. Her already wet pussy grew slick with arousal, and every part of her ached with the need to be touched.

He lowered his hands to the neckline of her already-ruined dress and gripped it, tearing it down to her breasts with one powerful move. He moved his hands and repeated the motion. She shrugged out of the remains of the garment and let it fall to the floor.

"Gods, you are beautiful." Radek put his hands on her hips and dropped to his knees. He bowed his head to press an open-mouthed kiss to the rounded curve of her stomach as he drew her panties down her legs. He was gentle this time, trailing his fingers over her skin in a long, drawn-out caress that made her weak in the knees. He was a man at worship, and she was his goddess. It was the sexiest thing she'd ever experienced.

Once her panties reached her ankles, she stepped out of them, and took a few more steps until her back was against the nearest wall. The cool surface felt good against her overheated skin and helped her regain her sense of balance. She expected Radek would stand up and join her. Instead, he covered the distance between them on his knees. Without a word, he ran his hands up her legs, starting at her ankles and moving higher. When he reached her knees, he curved his fingers around her left leg, coaxing her to raise it.

Her cheeks were burning, but she did it, planting one hand flat against the wall as he carefully lifted her leg and draped it over his shoulder. He raised his head, and the look in his eyes was so scorching hot she was surprised the walls weren't already melting. She reached down to stroke his hair. "Whatever it is you want from me, the answer is yes. All you have to do is look at me the way you are right now, and the answer will always be yes."

His mouth curved up into a predatory smile that showed just a hint of fang. "I want everything. Your body, your mind, and eventually, *sadina*, I intend to claim your heart. You. Are. Mine."

She didn't have time to react to his words before his face was buried between her thighs, and once his tongue touched her clit, she lost the ability to speak at all. He went slowly at first, using his mouth and fingers to explore her body and learn what made her moan with delight. He was a quick learner, and soon he focused most of his attention on her clitoris, lapping at it with quick, hard strokes that left her trembling and breathless. She closed her eyes and sank into the glorious sensation of being devoured.

Every touch sent a cascade of sensations flowing through her, each one pushing her a little closer to orgasm. She rocked her hips against his mouth, riding his tongue and his long, talented fingers as he played her body like a maestro performing his favourite piece of music. It didn't take him long to take her to the brink, and then send her hurtling over it into a place of pure bliss. She came hard, crying out his name in long, drawn-out syllables. Too drunk on pleasure to stay upright any longer, she started to slide down the wall. Radek was on his feet in a second, catching her in his arms and cradling her close to his chest.

"Too much?" he asked, a note of concern in his voice.

"Hell, no. That was perfect. Ten out of ten, with bonus points for the finish."

He uttered a deep chuckle that rolled over her like summer thunder. "I liked the finish, too. Next time, we'll finish together."

"Sounds good. We can do that just as soon as my legs start working."

"You don't need your legs to work for what I have in mind." He lifted her into his arms and headed for a raised platform at the back of the room.

There was a single handle set into the outer wall, and several square rainforest-style shower heads set into the ceiling. At least, that's what she thought they were. She'd never seen plumbing made of ice before.

"Won't those melt?" she asked as he stepped onto the platform.

"When I was still learning to control my powers, that might have been a problem, but I've had more than thirty years of practice. I promise you, nothing is going to melt until it's time for us to leave this place."

"More than thirty years, huh? How old are you, anyway?" He looked like he was in his late twenties, the same as her.

He planted himself in the center of the platform and glanced up. A moment later a gentle flow of perfectly heated water started raining down on them both. "Too hot?"

"Perfect. And you haven't answered my question."

He grinned. "I was trying to do the math. I am approximately fifty of your years, though by the standards of my people, I'm still quite young." His expression darkened for a moment. "Especially if those people are members of my family."

"Sounds like we have that in common, old man." Piper leaned in and kissed him as the water flowed over her like a sensual caress. Her senses were all so heightened, even a shower was an erotic experience.

He kissed her back, letting her slide down his body as he set her gently back on her feet without letting go. He reached out and dipped his hand into an alcove in the wall she hadn't noticed before. "For cleaning," he murmured between kisses. He placed a hand on her back, smoothing something thicker and cooler than the water over her skin. She reached up to the same nook and dipped her fingers inside. It felt like liquid soap. She withdrew her hand and held it under her nose. It smelled of fruit and green growing things, like an orchard after it rained.

She smoothed her hands over his broad chest, following the lines of muscle that flowed beneath his skin. He released her and raised his head, moving his hands to mirror hers. She wanted to move slowly and enjoy these moments, but she couldn't resist moving her hands ever lower. When she reached the base of his cock he groaned her name, cupping his hand over her mons, one finger pressed to the seam of her pussy.

She curled her fingers around his thick shaft and pumped him slowly, feeling the way the hard ridges moved beneath her palm. She cupped his sac in her other hand, and he responded by sliding one long finger inside her folds to press against the swollen nub of her clit.

"Don't stop. I need your hands on me."

"I have no intention of stopping." She slid one finger between his thighs to tease the tender flesh hidden behind his balls. He hissed in pleasure, his hips jerking in her hand as his cock swelled, the ridges growing more pronounced.

"Thank the Gods for that, because I'm not sure I'd survive it if you stopped now." He started slowly fucking her with his fingers as he reached up to tangle the fingers of his free hand in her hair, pulling her in close enough to brand her lips with another kiss.

Pleasure bloomed deep inside her, expanding until there was nothing but the two of them locked together in a sensual give-and-take that didn't end until they were both panting and shaking with need.

***

His mate was pure perfection. He'd been looking for her for so long he had started to wonder if the priests were right. They had told him that the Gods would not produce his mate until he stopped advocating for change in defiance of the Gods' will. They'd been wrong about her, just as they had been wrong about everything else.

He withdrew his hand from between her thighs and reached down to tap her leg. "Up."

She reacted immediately, an act of unquestioning trust that was as arousing as her passionate kisses. He slid his hand behind her knee and used his other hand to cup her ass, lifting her into the air as he walked them both backwards until she was pressed against the back wall of the shower. She locked her legs around his waist and set her hands on his shoulders.

"Tell me who you belong to," he murmured as he moved into position, their bodies meshing together perfectly.

"Again?" she asked, laughing.

"Every day from now until death claims us," he vowed, and his dragon growled in agreement.

"You're going to get bored of hearing it long before that happens."

"Never." In time, she would come to understand that the bond between them would never fade. Their lives and their souls were intertwined, and when they died, they would take their last breath together.

Piper's smile dimmed for a split second. "Never say never, lover. The universe tends to punish that kind of arrogance."

There was a story behind her statement, but now wasn't the time for talking. Now was the moment he truly claimed her as his own. He arched his hips, siding the tip of his cock into the welcoming heat of her body. "It's not arrogance, it's destiny."

She dug her nails into his shoulders and kissed him with a wild, desperate passion that snapped the last vestiges of his control. He surged into her, burying himself hilt deep. After that, they were both undone, lost in the wonder of each other's bodies. The sounds of their lovemaking filled the room – the slap of wet flesh coming together, soft moans, and breathless whispers of encouragement.

He lifted her higher, giving himself more space to move. His thrusts came hard and fast, pounding into her with more power than he'd ever allowed himself with any other lover. He was one with the wildest parts of his nature, near-feral in his need for her. Without thinking he lowered his head, pressing his mouth to the spot where her shoulder and neck met. He ran the point of one fang over the spot and she shivered, one hand lifting from his shoulder to cup the back of his head, pulling him even closer.

He nipped her sharply and she moaned aloud, her inner walls gripping his cock tight. Stars exploded in his vision and he had to fight the urge to sink his fangs into her neck. She was newly converted, and he had no idea if his love bite would bring her pleasure or pain. He couldn't risk hurting her, so he lifted his head and kissed her again, fucking her mouth in time to the pounding rhythm of his strokes.

They rose to the heights of pleasure together, racing toward release, urging each other higher, harder, and faster until he threw back his head and roared as his orgasm hit with all the force of a winter storm. Her release came seconds after his, her body shuddering as she milked his cock through his final thrusts.

Afterward, she sagged in his arms, her head on his shoulder and her breath coming in ragged gasps as she clung to him weakly. He held her close and moved them back to the center of the platform, letting the hot water flow over them both.

Eventually, she stirred, lifting her head to look at him with a contented smile. "I think you broke me. I don't want to move."

He lifted her gently, just enough to separate their bodies, then settled her back into his arms. "Then stay right where you are until you're ready."

"You have no idea how sexy it is that you can hold

me up like this and not make any comments about the fact I need to go on a diet."

"Why would I do that? You are perfect just as you are."

"Congratulations, you made yourself even sexier with that question. Are there more of you back on Romak? I can think of a few friends who would kill for a guy like you." Her eyes narrowed. "But only ones *like* you. You are spoken for."

"Yes, I am, may Solun and Daga be praised. You are the proof I came to Earth to find, and so much more."

"Proof? Of what?"

"That is a conversation that should wait until we are dry and comfortable. There is a great deal I need to tell you."

"Any chance this conversation can be had while we eat?" She frowned. "What are we going to eat, anyway? There's nothing around here but berries and tree bark."

He arched a brow at her and grinned. "You're welcome to eat tree bark if you wish, but I intend to dine properly."

"And how do you intend to do that, exactly? Even if I had my phone, I'm betting Domino's doesn't deliver to the middle of nowhere, second pine tree on the right."

"I love how quickly you've come to accept things that were beyond your imagining less than an hour ago. I created everything around us, remember? If you are hungry, I'll conjure us a meal."

Instead of looking impressed, Piper looked

crestfallen. "You can just summon up a meal anytime you want to?"

"It requires focus, and the right spell of course, but, yes, I can. You said you were hungry, why aren't you pleased I can provide us with food?"

"I'm a chef, Radek. Preparing food is the only thing in the world I'm good at." She pushed lightly at his chest. "You can put me down now."

He had no intention of letting go of her, not when she was clearly unhappy. "I don't understand. Did you wish to prepare our meal? Is this a human courtship custom?"

"Normally, yes. Cooking dinner for someone is part of getting to know them, but that's not going to happen, considering I don't even have a stove to cook on. The thing is, you keep saying I'm your mate. That implies we're a couple, which means either you're staying on Earth, or I'm going to your world, right? How am I going to earn a living if everyone can just wave a hand and conjure themselves a six-course meal?"

"I see."

She poked his chest. "Still not putting me down or answering my question."

"I don't want to put you down, though I suppose that's going to have to happen soon, or we'll both be waterlogged. As for your question, I apologize. I was marvelling at the fact you are worried what you'll do for money, *mila*. I am a prince, remember? As my mate, you are entitled to all I have." He kissed the tip of her nose. "As it happens, that's more than the two of us could spend in a hundred lifetimes."

"Prince. Right. The whole dragon thing bumped that fact off my radar. Still, what am I going to do all day? I'm not really the pampered princess type, and what's a *mila*?"

He carried her out of the shower and over to where a collection of thick towels sat. Setting her back on her feet, he took the topmost towel and offered it to her. "A *mila* is a flower or blossom. And if you wish to cook, you can. Like everything else, magic has limitations. It takes energy and focus to cast a spell. While I can conjure all we'll need for the next few days, I wouldn't want to rely on magic forever. Besides, there is no spell in existence that could recreate an Earth meal, because no one on Romak has ever eaten one."

Piper's eyes lit up. "That's right! If I opened a restaurant based on Earth cuisine, I'd be the only game in town. Hell, the only one on the planet. Any rules about members of the royal family serving meals to other people…uh…beings?"

"None. All my family have jobs and duties of one kind or another. If that would make you happy, then I see no reason not to do it." The priests would disapprove, of course, but what could they do? Their influence would start to wane the moment he returned home and introduced Piper at court. She was proof that the priests' warnings were fearmongering and their laws nothing more than lies to benefit the temple.

She towelled herself off, looking much happier now.

"If all your family members have duties, what are yours?"

He shrugged. "That depends on who you ask. My parents would tell you I consider it my sworn duty to challenge the status quo, the temples, and the traditions upon which our society was built. I'd say that I'm a student of history and the self-appointed diplomatic liaison for off-world visitors. Not that there's much call for diplomacy these days. The last group to arrive on Romak for trade talks were sent packing after only a few days."

"So, you're the black sheep of your family, too, huh?"

He rubbed a towel over his hair then tossed it into a corner, where it promptly disappeared. "I'm not familiar with that expression. Black sheep?"

"You're the family member who doesn't fit in with the others, right? The one who thinks and acts differently. We have that in common."

Piper flicked a lock of her hair, then stuck out her tongue to show him her piercing. "My sister loves me, but she doesn't understand me. She used to try so hard to make me more like her, but the harder she pushed, the more I fought back."

"You have just described my relationship with my parents perfectly." He opened his arms to her and she walked into his embrace, wrapping her arms around his waist and laying her head on his chest. Frost and Fire, he liked holding her. It soothed his soul, and his dragon, in a way he'd never experienced before. "You used the past tense when you talked about fighting with your sister. Have you two stopped fighting? What about your parents? You haven't mentioned them. Didn't they try and keep the peace between you?"

She uttered a soft sigh. "My parents are both gone. My father passed on when I was still a baby, and Mum died when I was a teenager. Aria basically raised me, and I didn't make it easy for her. We are getting better at communicating, now." Piper laughed and shook her head. "Though she lost her mind a little today when I told her my new job was cancelled because the restaurant burned down. If she knew I'd damned near died and then been abducted by a space dragon, she'd probably try to seal me in a room full of bubble wrap for the rest of my life."

"I'm sorry to hear about your parents. Mine drive me to distraction, but I cannot imagine what it would be like to lose them."

"Losing mom sucked. Everyone kept telling me I'd get over her death eventually, but they lied. I'll miss her every day for the rest of my life. It's just that now the grief is quiet, more like a whisper than a roar that drowns out the rest of the world."

He kissed the crown of her hair. His *sadina* had suffered more grief in her short life than he could imagine. "If there is ever a moment it becomes a roar again, tell me. I will do what I can to help you get through it."

"Thank you." She lifted her head and gave him a smile that filled his heart with light. "Just being like this, with you, it helps. I feel different. Complete. And I cannot believe I said that out loud." Her cheeks turned a brilliant pink, and she dropped her head back to his chest. "Sorry for being such a sap. I'm going to blame the whole mating fever thing for this, too."

"If I were to confess that the world seems a better place now that I have you in my arms, that would also be the fault of the *rux*."

She peeked up at him. "You're adorable."

"I'm glad you think so, though if anyone else tried to describe me that way, I might have to freeze them solid."

"You can do that?"

He waggled his brows, enjoying himself and their conversation. "I'm a snow dragon, remember? Freezing things is kind of my thing."

"Too bad you weren't around yesterday. You could have put out the fire that ruined my chances of gainful employment."

"You won't be needing that job, anyway. Not if you come to Romak with me. I know that leaving your family and home won't be easy, but I—"

She cut him off with a wave of her hand. "I'm coming with you. I signed my sister and myself up for Star-Crossed Dating because I hoped one of us might find a good man who would love us and take us far, far away so I could live my life without her well-meaning interference. That's why I was at the stadium today, to support her. This might be the *rux* talking again, but the way I see it, you're offering me a chance to travel to a distant planet and live like a princess. I'd be a fool not to go."

"Not *like* a princess. As one. And what do you mean, you signed up with Star-Crossed? You wanted to be matched to a Pyrosian?" His last words came out as more of a growl as his dragon made his opinion known.

"Sexy aliens looking for love?" She shrugged, but her eyes were bright with laughter. "I figured it was worth a shot. I wasn't matched, though. It turns out, I was destined for a different sexy alien."

He hauled her up against his body, hands on her ass, holding her in close. "You were. I will have your information scrubbed from the Star-Crossed database the moment we are back onboard the *Firebrand*. You are no longer available to be matched."

"But what if I get a Pyrosian match, too? I've always wanted to have a threesome."

"No. No threesomes. No sharing. You are mine!" He picked her up and placed her over his shoulder, then smacked her bare ass cheek.

"Hey! I thought you were going to conjure us up something to eat?" She protested as he marched back into the main room and headed straight for the bed.

"Food later. Sex now."

"Words good. Use more?" she retorted, kicking her feet and raining a flurry of playful blows across his back.

"There are only a few words I want to hear from you for the next while. Yes, more, Radek, please, and mine."

"What about threesome, sharing, and Pyrosian-match?"

He growled and slapped her ass again. "You're playing with fire, *sadina*."

"Really? I thought you were a snow dragon?"

He was grinning as he made it to the bed and tossed her into the middle of it, then pounced on top of her, pinning her easily. "You're incredibly sexy when you sass me. Promise me you'll never stop doing that."

Her joyful laughter filled the room and echoed off the walls. "Now, that's a promise I know I can keep."

CHAPTER FIVE

PIPER HAD NEVER BEEN HAPPIER in her entire life. Part of it was because of Radek, and the rest was because the *rux* wouldn't let her think about anything unpleasant for very long. Focusing on anything for more than a few minutes was like trying to hold onto a handful of sand. No matter how hard she tried, everything kept slipping away from her. Everything but Radek. They'd only been together for a single day, but he was already part of her, woven into her psyche and branded onto her senses. She knew his scent, the taste of his mouth, the low rumbling growl he made when his dragon was making his presence known. She had fallen asleep to the lullaby of his heartbeat and woken up feeling energized and eager to meet the day. Not even the lack of coffee put a dent in her good mood.

"What did you say this was?" she asked as Radek handed her a mug of steaming, dark- red liquid.

"*Korta*. I believe you'll find it contains a similar stimulant to the coffee you described to me."

She took a tentative sip and held it in her mouth long enough to appreciate the flavour. It reminded her of black tea, only there were subtle notes of fruit, too. She swallowed and took another, bigger sip before nodding at him with approval. "This is good. Is your friend Vadir trying to export this stuff to Earth? I bet he'd make a killing."

Radek had told her about Vadir's attempts to expand trade with his planet. She still didn't understand exactly why the Romaki rulers and the priests were so averse to the idea of connecting with other races. In the short period of time Earth had been an intergalactic trading partner, the world had changed so much. New technology, better medical treatments, massive advances in humanity's understanding of the universe and space travel, and even a few new foods and luxury items had appeared recently, though they were far too pricey for her to even consider on her limited budget.

"If he thought he could make money selling it here, it's on his list. He talked about Earth, the new markets and potential for trade for the entire voyage here. That male is obsessed."

"We're all passionate about something. For me, it's food. I've bored my sister to tears talking about meal preparation or the latest trends in fine dining, and while she was studying to become a psychologist, she drove me crazy talking about diagnoses and treatments for mental disorders I'd never even heard of." Piper took another sip, then added, "I bet your family members start looking pained the moment you start talking about ancient history and Romaki legends."

He nodded. "They do, but not because I talk about it at length. I learned long ago that what I consider fascinating is quite different from what the rest of my family enjoys discussing. I told you my family thinks of me as the rebellious child who refuses to grow up and accept things as they are. It's..." He sighed and scrubbed a hand through his hair. "It's a little more complicated than that. My species worship two gods. Solun, Lord of Frost, and Daga, Mistress of Flame. There was a time when their priests were content to focus on spiritual matters and didn't seek to influence the leaders of the two clans or interfere with the laws that ruled us. That changed after the Romaki started to travel to other worlds. I've studied the forbidden and forgotten texts. I know what really happened, but the priests have so much influence now, my parents chose to believe them over their own son."

There was so much pain in his final statement it made her want to meet his parents just so she could smack them. She rose from the table and went around to Radek, wrapping her arms around his shoulders and pressing her cheek to his. "Your parents are idiots. I know I should probably not mention that to them the first time we meet, what with the fact they're dragons and I'm just a crunchy human that would taste good with ketchup, but I'm tempted to tell them so, anyway."

"You're not –wait, what? Crunchy? ketchup?"

He sounded so perplexed she burst into a fit of giggles. "It's an expression. 'Do not mess in the affairs of dragons, for you are crunchy and taste good with ketchup. It's a tangy sauce lots of people use as a condiment."

"We don't eat our enemies. That's disgusting. It's so much tidier to just freeze them or burn them to ash."

"Oh yeah, that makes me feel so much better about meeting your parents. What if they hate me? I'm not even the right species for you. Shit. The priests you were talking about. They're not going to like me much, either, are they?"

He turned his head and kissed her. "You are my mate, the female the Gods chose for me. No one would dare harm you, and the only one with plans to devour you is me."

"You're welcome to devour me anytime you like, my sexy dragon prince." She was still wrapping her head around the fact that Radek was everything he'd claimed to be, and so much more. A dragon. A prince. A magic user. A talented and breathtakingly thorough lover, and a man who made her feel like she was the center of his universe. They were only starting to get to know each other, but each time she had doubts, a little voice would whisper that all would be well, that he was hers, and that was all she needed to believe.

"Promise me that I won't have to face the priests, or your parents, alone. I can face anything, even cranky dragon-in-laws, if you're with me."

"I promise. Whatever comes, we'll face it together, my *sadina*."

There was still so much they needed to talk about. She had dozens of questions about his family, his life on Romak, and what it would be like to live there, but it all started to slip away again. Even her frustration at her lack of focus only lasted a few seconds, and then she was sliding her hands down Radek's bare chest as she nibbled his earlobe. She'd discovered that his ears were just the slightest bit pointed at the top, and she'd been fascinated with them ever since.

"If you keep that up, I'll be carrying you back to bed soon," he warned her.

"That's my cunning plan. Glad it's working."

"As happy as the thought of loving you makes me, I had thought that it might be nice to get out of here for a little while before the *rux* returns."

"Out where? There's nothing around for kilometres, remember?"

"I do. Which is why it would be quite safe for me to stretch my wings and take you flying. Last time we flew you were in no shape to appreciate the experience."

"Yes! Oh my god, yes, yes, yes! I'd love that." She let go of him to do a gleeful little dance that ended with her landing in a laughing tangle in his lap. She was dying to see him as a dragon again.

"So, that's a yes?" he was laughing as he looked down at her.

"Oh yeah. I'm going to be a dragon rider!" She frowned. "I am going to be on your back, right? Not dangling from your claws like your next involuntary meal?"

He wrinkled his nose in distaste. "Your legends really haven't portrayed my species accurately. Why would I carry off some poor herd beast to eat when I can summon a decent, well-prepared meal any time I'm hungry?"

"For the same reason you dragons got accused of abducting every village virgin you could get your claws on. It makes for a better story."

"Only if you're not the dragon," he pointed out.

"Good point. We'll have to set the record straight. We should probably wait until after people know you exist, though."

His lips twisted into a wry grin. "I suspect your people are already aware of my existence. I did transform in the middle of the stadium and fly off in full view of anyone who happened to be looking up at the time."

"Subtle."

"I was distracted by the near-death of my mate and the need to get both of us somewhere private. Still, I'm sure I will have a lot to answer for when we return to the *Firebrand*. I gave my word I would not shapeshift while I was on Earth."

"Everyone was probably too busy running from the explosions to notice you, and even if they did see something, you'd be amazed how good humans are at ignoring things we can't easily explain."

"If I was seen, then I'll accept the consequences. Protecting you will always be my first priority."

"I know, and I think it's sexy as hell. I've never had a protector before, and man, I really could have used a badass dragon boyfriend back in high school."

"I suspect your sister would not have approved of me." He frowned. "Do you think she'll have trouble accepting our mating? If she is as protective of you as you say she is, she may resent the fact I'm taking you away from her."

"Oh, she'll be grumpy about it, but it's not her life or her choice. There will be ways for us to communicate, right? Even if I'm on a different planet?"

"Of course."

"Then it will be fine, eventually. Everyone is going to need a period of adjustment, but we'll figure it out." After all, they were mated. This was their destiny, as sanctioned by some ancient dragon Gods. Who was she to argue with that?

***

RADEK NEEDED to tell Piper the truth about what her arrival would herald, and why. She was the first dragon-mate to be converted and claimed in centuries, a sign from Solun and Daga themselves that the destiny of the Romaki dragon clans waited for them out among the stars.

He also had to tell Piper that she was no longer human, but a dragon. At least, he thought she was. So little information had survived the temple's purges he couldn't be sure of anything. Frost and Fire, he hadn't even been certain his bite would trigger the conversion and save her life. From what he remembered of the texts about converted mates, if she were fully converted, her dragon should manifest herself soon. If that happened before he could explain… He made his decision. First, he'd take her flying, then he'd tell her. It would be easier for her to accept once she was more familiar with his dragon form, wouldn't it?

"We will figure it out, together." He kissed her forehead. "Come, *sadina*. I need to stretch my wings."

Tempted as he was to have her ride him naked, he conjured a simple dress and a cloak for her to wear as protection against the wind and cold.

She dressed in seconds and headed for the door with a bounce in her step and a gleeful smile on her face. "Let's go, dragon man."

Once outside, he gestured for her to stay back as he moved to the centre of the clearing. The sun was warm, the grass soft beneath his bare feet, and the air was full of birdsong. It was a beautiful day, and he raised his face to the sky to give a silent prayer of thanks to the Gods for bringing him to this place. After a lifetime of dreaming of other worlds, he was finally standing on one. Even more amazing, he had found his mate here. It was a lot to be grateful for.

"As much as I'm enjoying the view, is there a reason you're still a naked sexy man instead of a sexy dragon?" Piper called out.

"I was enjoying the moment and thanking the Gods for my beautiful, if rather impatient, mate."

Her only response was a riff of laughter that blended with the songs of the birds and insects.

Radek closed his eyes, exhaled, and summoned his dragon. The beast arrived with a roar that shattered the serenity of the forest.

"Nice entrance. I think you scared the wildlife for ten miles around."

He rumbled in response. It was the only communication he could manage for now. Mates and family members could speak mind-to-mind, but only in dragon form. He stretched out on the grass and watched as she approached. There was no hesitation this time. She walked up to his head and pressed a kiss to his scaled cheek. "I should not be turned on by the fact you just turned into a giant, winged reptile, but dammit, I am. You are gorgeous in any form."

He moved his head the slightest bit, bumping her gently. It was as close as he could come to an affectionate touch.

Piper walked slowly down his side, letting her hand trail over his body as she made her way to his foreleg. "You know, this sounded simple when you explained it to me inside. But now I'm not so sure. How the hell am I supposed to get from your claw to your back? I swear I don't remember you being this big."

He raised his claw, then lowered it again, reminding her of the plan.

"Right. Up I go." She gathered her skirt and cloak in

one hand and clambered onto his forelimb, cursing with remarkable creativity the whole time.

Once she had her balance, he raised his claw as high as he could, then swung his tail around, so the tip was within easy reach.

"Oh, I get it now." She caught hold of his tail with both hands and grinned. "Upsie-daisy."

He lifted her the rest of the way, settling her on his back with care. It was the first time he'd carried another being this way, and it was both strange and slightly erotic to have his mate's bare legs straddling him, her hands resting on the dorsal ridge just in front of her.

He turned to look back at her, and she beamed, holding one hand out with her thumb sticking up. "Let's go!"

He rose slowly, unfurled his wings, and launched himself into the air. She yelped and clung to him but didn't lose her seat. After a few strokes of his wings her grip eased, and by the time they were a hundred meters off the ground, she was whooping with delight.

"This is amazing!" she shouted. "Take us higher."

Her joy was infectious. He did as she asked, soaring in wide circles as he continued to climb. The lush forest was a deep green sea beneath them, rising and falling with the hills. Lakes and rivers sparkled like sun-struck gems among the green, and the sky overhead was a brilliant blue, so different than the deep lapis skies of Romak.

His wild little mate drummed her heels against his sides, and he glanced back to see she had her arms outstretched so her cloak billowed out behind her like a sail. She was red-cheeked and laughing into the wind. He folded his wings, dropping into a dive. She cheered, laughed, and then suddenly her laughter stopped, and she grabbed hold of him again, clinging to his back so tightly he could feel her shaking.

He pulled out of the dive and made for the nearest landing site he could find, an open stretch of scrubland beside a small lake. He landed by the water's edge, not bothering to lower her from her perch before changing forms. A few seconds later he was lying on the ground, naked, with Piper sitting on his back.

"What's wrong?" he demanded the second he could speak.

She got to her feet, swaying slightly. "I don't know. Everything was fine until you went into that dive. Then I had this insane urge to jump off your back and try to fly on my own."

Uh oh. He rose and went to her, wrapping her in his arms. She leaned against him, still shaking. "You're safe, *sadina*. I'll be more careful on the way back. No more dives." *Or anything else that might tempt her newly waking dragon to test her wings.*

"That's not all of it." She leaned her head back to look up at him with wide eyes. "I heard a…a voice. Inside my head."

"What did she say?"

"Free." Her eyes narrowed. "And how the hell did you know it was a woman's voice I heard?"

So much for telling her when the time was right. He

was going to have to tell her now and hope she forgave him.

Piper didn't know what the fuck was going on, but she had a feeling Radek did. The longer he stood without speaking, the more certain she was that whatever he finally said, she wasn't going to like it.

"When I found you, you were dying."

"I know. You told me. But you healed me. I'm fine. At least, I thought I was. Is this some freaky side effect of dying?"

"It's a side effect of my healing you." Radek sighed and cupped her cheek in his hand. "I didn't know if it would work at all, but it did. Even then, I wasn't sure that this would happen. I hoped…"

She moved her head back, away from his touch. She needed to be thinking clearly right now, and every time they touched, her brain tended to shut down. "What is it? What did you do to me, Radek?"

"I bit you. It's how my species claim our mates."

"So what, I have dragon rabies? Why would you hope for that?"

"You don't have rabies. You do, however, have a dragon." He gave a frustrated growl. "I'm not explaining this very well."

"You really aren't. All I've got so far is that you bit me. Not thrilled about that. You also claimed me as your mate while I was unconscious. Really not happy about that either. And now I have a dragon?" A jolt of panic hit her as she worked out a possible explanation. "Son of a bitch. Don't you dare tell me you got me pregnant! I am not ready to be a mother. Especially not a dragon baby momma!"

"No! You're not pregnant. At least, I don't think you are. Can humans tell that quickly?"

"I'm on the pill, so I shouldn't be pregnant, but I don't know how freaky dragon sex-magic interacts with human pharmaceuticals. How could I?" Her hands were fluttering in the air like a pair of drunk hummingbirds as she gestured to him, then herself. "If I'm not pregnant, or infected with some dragon disease, then why do I hear voices?"

"You do not hear voices. You hear one voice. Her voice. Your dragon has emerged."

"My…" She stopped and stared at him. "Say that again."

"You are hearing the voice of your dragon. When I bit you, I converted you from your species to mine. It was the only way to save you."

"I'm not *human*?" She was reeling from information overload.

"You're still partially human. At least, I believe you are. There hasn't been a mating like ours in centuries. The priests tried to destroy any proof it was even possible, but I found some references. It wasn't much, but it was enough for me to know it was possible. I had to try. I regret that it was done without your permission. I asked for your forgiveness even as I did it, but I was trying to save your life."

"Let go of me." She needed a moment to herself to process everything.

"Piper I need—"

She shoved at his chest, ignoring the part of her that wanted to burrow deeper into his arms, not push him away. "You need to let me go, now!"

He released her. "Sorry."

"You should be! You turned me into a dragon and didn't tell me, Radek! We really need to work on your communication skills. Is there anything else I should know?" Not that she was in any state to cope with more weird news right now, but she'd rather be overwhelmed now than ambushed later.

His expression turned sheepish. "I mentioned that the priests and leaders of my world believe it's safer for my species to stay on the planet and not interact too much with other races. What I didn't tell you is that it's actually forbidden for any Romaki to leave the planet."

"But you did."

"I did. I broke the law and left with Vadir after my mother cancelled the trade talks. My family doesn't know where I am, though by now they will suspect I'm no longer on my homeworld."

Anger and uncertainty pooled in her stomach in a toxic stew. She tried to speak, but instead of words, she uttered a low, rumbling growl as the voice in her head spoke again, much louder this time. *"Protect."*

She grabbed her head. "Ow."

"Your dragon?" he asked.

"Is very loud and convinced we need to protect you. What do you need protection from, and why does my damned dragon seem to know more about this than I do? Will they try and punish you for breaking the law? That's not going to happen. You're my mate, and I'm the only one who gets to dole out punishments."

His expression changed from apologetic to one of relief, which annoyed her. She wasn't done being mad at him, yet. "Why are you looking so relieved? You're still in trouble."

He gave her a devilish grin. "I'm used to being in trouble. I'm not used to having someone around to defend me."

"Well, get used to it. You bit me, so you're stuck with me," she said.

"Protect. Ours," her dragon growled, and this time Piper agreed with her.

"Oh, for the love of—yes, he's ours. Now shut up, I'm trying to get a handle on this, and you're not helping." She looked at Radek. "Are all dragons this chatty?"

He was trying not to laugh as he nodded. "They do like to have their say. You don't have to answer her out loud, though."

"Right. Because that would just make me look crazy. Who is going to believe I'm actually possessed by a dragon?"

"Not possessed. She's part of you." He patted his

bare chest. "They're our most primal instincts and impulses made manifest."

"Oh shit. My sister is always saying I have an impulse control problem. Does this mean that part of me now has a mind of its own?"

"Indeed. And wings, and access to magic."

Piper groaned. "Great. I'm a potential weapon of mass destruction. One bout of PMS and oops, there goes the city."

"You're not going to hurt anyone. I'll teach you how to control her if you'll let me."

He reached for her, and this time she didn't move away.

"Need." Her dragon's voice was softer this time.

"Yeah, I know." It was hard to argue with the beast when it was only echoing what she already felt. It wasn't only the *rux* that had her craving Radek's touch. It was something deeper and far more powerful. How had he put it? Their souls recognized each other. It sounded corny, but it explained what she was feeling, and why she trusted him despite the fact he'd turned her life upside down. She hadn't forgiven him for keeping secrets, but she already knew she would.

She put her arms around him and hugged him tightly. "I'm going to need your help figuring all of this out. You got me into this mess. It seems only fair you help me deal with the consequences."

"Some of those consequences are quite amazing." He nuzzled her hair. "Would my *sadina* like to see what she looks like as a dragon?"

"Hell yes!" Her answer was accompanied by a rumbling note of approval from her beast.

"Then you won't be needing these." He flicked the fingers of his right hand, and her clothing vanished, leaving her naked in his arms.

"I'm going to save a fortune on clothing once I learn that trick."

"You're mated to a member of royalty, remember? I can afford to buy you anything your heart desires."

"It's going to be easier to wrap my head around the fact that I'm a dragon than it is to remember that I don't have to worry about money anymore." She rose up on her toes to kiss him. "So, how exactly do I turn into a dragon?"

His answer was delayed for several long, delightful minutes as he responded to her kiss with several of his own. By the time he was done, she was almost ready to postpone her lesson in favour of another round of mind-melting sex. The only thing stopping her was her dragon, who expressed her opinion firmly and at full volume. *Me first. Claim later.*

"Great. Not only is she pushy and loud, but my dragon's priorities are screwy," she muttered.

Radek chuckled, brushed a kiss to her cheek, and released her. "My dragon is in league with yours. He wants to see her, too."

"Okay. I guess it's time to give them what they want. How do I do this?"

"Wait until I'm far enough away, then close your

eyes and speak to your beast. Invite her to step forward. She'll take it from there."

"Uh huh. And how do I change back?" she asked, proud of herself for remembering to ask before she lost the ability to talk.

"Ask her to step back and imagine yourself in your current form. Oh, and while it won't hurt, it does feel exceedingly weird the first time you shift."

"This whole thing feels weird. I'm standing naked by a lake in the middle of the woods, trying to summon my overly opinionated spirit animal."

Radek moved farther up the shoreline, then turned back towards her. "Show me your dragon, *sadina*."

She closed her eyes, balled her hands into fists, and spoke to the creature who now dwelled inside her. *"Let's do this."*

CHAPTER SIX

RADEK HAD NEVER WITNESSED someone's first transformation. It was usually a private moment with only a few family members present. His father had been there for his first time, but his mother had been too busy. She'd attended the party afterward, though. He remembered because she had told him she loved him and was proud of him. It was the last time he could remember her saying that. He looked at Piper, standing alone on the shore, and he knew without a doubt that she would always be there for him.

He felt the pulse of magic a half-second before she shifted. Her power was strong. Stronger even than it had been when she'd come back to life in his arms. After that initial thought, he was too busy appreciating her new form to think of anything else.

From the delicate lines of silver that marked her muzzle to the tip of her iridescent blue and silver tail, she was perfect. She stretched out her neck and bugled so loudly flocks of birds rose from the trees in panicked flight, then unfurled her wings, stretching them out and flapping them slowly.

"Don't you even think about trying to fly, yet," he called out.

She swung her head in his direction and snorted in defiance.

"It's not the flying that I'm worried about. It's the landing. We need a much larger space for your first attempt." He walked over to her and waited for her to lower her head down to his level.

When she did, he stroked her cheek. "You are beautiful."

Her eye lit with pleasure, and she rumbled deep in her chest as she nudged him with her head, almost sending him flying. "You see? You're bigger and far stronger in this form. You'll have to get used to this body before we start your flying lessons."

Her eyes intrigued him. They were still blue, a trait that would mark her as unique among his kind. Romaki only had two eye colours, which were dictated by the source of their magic. Snow dragons had silver eyes, while the eyes of fire dragons were gold. Blue eyes were unheard of…until now.

She didn't stay still for long, and he stepped back to give her room to examine her new body. She looked at every part of herself she could, twisting her long neck this way and that as she checked everything from talons to tail.

"If you walk into the water, you should be able to

see your reflection," he suggested when she had finished her preliminary inspection.

She bobbed her head, then headed to the lake. Once her back was turned, he shifted shapes, too. He hadn't planned on it, but his dragon was insistent. *"There. Happy now?"*

"Yes," the beast replied with smug satisfaction.

He joined Piper in the lake, watching as his approach sent ripples chasing across the water's surface. *"Can you hear me?"* He sent the thought from his mind to hers.

Piper's head snapped up. *"Whoa. We can talk now?"*

"When we're both in dragon form, yes."

"Must get noisy when everyone's in dragon form. That's a lot of voices in your head."

He couldn't remember the last time he'd talked to another being this way. Usually, he shifted forms to escape, not to socialize. *"I prefer to fly alone."*

"Not anymore. You've got a wingman – uh, wingwoman to fly with you now. Remember what I said. You bit me, so you're stuck with me."

"Best decision I ever made." He extended one of his wings, draping it over her back.

"I think so, too." Piper twined her neck with his, and the two of them stood like that for a long time, basking in the sun and enjoying the moment. In a few days, they'd have to return to the *Firebrand* and eventually to Romak, where Piper's arrival would finally prove to everyone, especially his family, that he'd been right all along.

It was the *rux* that forced Piper to change back to human form. Even the cool lake water wasn't enough to quench the mating fever that was starting to build again. She forgot to leave the water before she changed back, though, and the sudden plunge left her spluttering and soaked as she stomped back to shore.

Radek followed close behind her, though he didn't shift until he was on the shore. "Sorry. I should have reminded you to get to dry land before shifting. The change in size will take some getting used to."

"Yeth it doth." She stopped dead. Something was screwy. A quick swipe of her tongue over her teeth revealed the problem. "Why do I haff fangs?"

"Show me," Radek said, looking pleased.

She bared her teeth, curling her upper lip back so he could see for himself.

"The change must have been triggered when you shifted to dragon form."

"You didn't mention fangs were part of the package." She slowed down and enunciated every word, so she didn't lisp this time.

"I didn't know it was possible." He stroked her cheek tenderly, but his eyes were burning with arousal.

"You cannot pothibly be turned on by this."

His brows rose to his hairline. "Why wouldn't I be? You can bite me now. Gods, I cannot wait to feel those pretty little fangs on my skin."

His words sent a torrent of images pouring through

her mind and her pulse raced and her body start to hum with sexual energy. Even her dragon liked the idea. *"Claim. Bite. Ours."*

"You're both nuts." It was getting easier to speak already.

"You're outnumbered, *sadina*. Three to one."

She threw up her hands in surrender. "If I'm being honest, I think your fangs are thex-sexy, too. And when you nibble on my neck…"

"What does that do to you? Tell me."

"I like it. A lot. And I keep thinking how good it would feel if you bit me," she confessed.

Radek groaned, then leaned down to kiss her, hauling her up against his naked body with a hunger that left her breathless. Tongues danced and limbs tangled as he lifted her into his arms and carried her away from the edge of the lake. She didn't know where they were going and really didn't care, either. She was lost in the *rux* again, adrift in a sea of pleasure without a care in the world.

They didn't go far. After only a minute or two of walking the sunlight suddenly dimmed and she opened her eyes to look around. They were under a canopy of hunter green, gossamer-thin fabric so light it fluttered in the slightest breeze, and the ground was covered with a thick blanket strewn with cushions.

"How'd you manage this? I didn't hear you chant or say so much as a hocus-pocus," she asked, waving a hand at the bower he'd created.

"Incantations create intent and help with focus, but

they're not always necessary. Especially if the task isn't complex." Radek knelt, then gently lowered her to the ground.

"So, one day I'll be able to make something like this appear out of thin air?" She contemplated the idea as she stretched out on the blanket, letting herself sink into the sumptuously soft cushions. She was going to be able to cast spells!

He stretched out beside her. "You will. I'll teach you. By the time we reach Romak, you'll need to have mastered at least a few spells."

"Why? Will they want to test me? Make sure I'm the real deal?" Some of her eagerness faded as another thought crossed her mind. "Or is this because I might need to know how to defend myself? The priests aren't going to like me, much. Right?

"They might dislike what your arrival means, but even the most difficult of them would never harm you. You will be safe. I swear it."

Questions rose in the back of her mind, but they popped like soap bubbles before she could focus long enough to ask any of them.

He leaned in and kissed her tenderly. "You are everything I dreamed of in a mate, and so much more. I hoped to spend my life with someone who understood and accepted me. I never considered that the Gods would send me someone strong enough to fight my battles at my side."

She touched her chest over her heart, then placed her hand flat against his chest. "I'm still working on understanding what's happened between us, but I don't need to understand it to accept that it's real. We're a team now, and that means that they're not your battles anymore. They're *ours*."

"Gods, I love you," he whispered before kissing her again. His mouth plundered hers as he covered her body with his, wedging a knee between her thighs as he moved over her.

She opened herself to him. Not just her body, but her heart, too. She couldn't say the words yet, she wasn't ready, but she recognized the truth. She was going to fall in love with this strange, wonderful man from another world. It was inevitable.

He kissed his way down her body, tasting and teasing her with his mouth and tongue until he reached her breasts. He sucked one taut nipple into his mouth, his fangs lightly denting her skin as he worked his tongue over the hard nub. His fingers worked her other nipple with the same rhythm, rolling it between his fingers until she was burning with need and rubbing herself against him everywhere she could reach. Her need for him was a physical ache that grew stronger with every passing moment.

She buried her fingers in his hair and pulled him closer, arching her back at the same time. He seemed to understand her need, because his touch grew rougher and he finally used his fangs, raking the tips across her nipple with just enough force to make her moan.

As good as she felt, she needed more, and she released his head to run her hands over his shoulders, feeling the muscles play beneath his skin. "This doesn't seem fair. You're doing all the work and I'm getting all the enjoyment."

He chuckled without releasing her breast from his mouth, and the vibrations of his laughter rolled through her.

"Please?" she said. That got his attention. He raised his head and gave her a heated look that nearly had her come on the spot.

"I swear, I'm enjoying this almost as much as you are, *sadina*, but if you wish to add to my pleasure, I'd be a fool to stop you."

She grinned at him. "You are definitely not a fool."

"Feel free to share that opinion with my family once we're home."

She lifted her head and bared her teeth. "Oh, believe me, I plan on it."

He was laughing as he moved off her, adjusting his position so that he was kneeling behind her head with his knees beside her ears. She caught on immediately, and by the time he was settled on his hands and knees, she was already raising her head to capture the head of his cock in her mouth. "Fangs," Radek reminded her, and she hummed in acknowledgement before running her piercing over the ridges of his cock. He groaned and thrust deeper into her mouth, and she shifted her jaw so that one fang stroked along his length each time he moved.

"Yes. Gods yes," he muttered, then bowed his head and pressed his mouth to the lips of her pussy. She gasped as his tongue slid inside, pinpointing her clit within seconds. Measured touches turned to urgent caresses, and soon they were caught up in a tempest of passion that had both of them moaning and grinding against each other as they pushed each other to their breaking points.

Determined to bring him to orgasm first, Piper hollowed her cheeks and sucked him deep into her mouth. He retaliated by drawing the tender nub of her clit into his mouth, lashing it with his tongue until stars exploded in her vision.

She flattened her tongue against the underside of his cock and opened wider, letting him fuck her mouth. His thighs tensed and his dick thickened, the ridges growing more pronounced as he neared the end of his control. Lust fogged her mind and tempted her to give in, but she hung on, not willing to break until he did. Her determination was paying off until Radek released her clit and turned his head. He nipped her thigh hard with his fangs at the same moment he slid two fingers into her channel, and she shattered into a thousand pieces of shimmering bliss.

He moved away from her while she was still too dazed to protest, and when she next opened her eyes, he was kneeling over her again, looking down with a self-satisfied smile.

"Cheater," she grumbled.

"You said you wanted me to bite you. You didn't say when to do it."

She stuck her tongue out before replying. "I'm going to make you regret those words."

His grin widened. "You have no idea how much I'm looking forward to that moment. But for the moment, I have a more pressing need, mate. Up on your hands and knees."

"This is your plan to keep my pointy teeth away from your sexy bod so I can't seek my revenge, isn't it?"

"Trust me," was his cryptic response, but it was accompanied by one of his sexy smiles. It hadn't taken him long to figure out that when he smiled at her like that she'd agree to damn near anything.

"You know I do." She rose into position, turning away from him and spreading her legs. He moved in behind her, stroking his hands down her ass to the slick folds of her pussy.

"I know, *sadina*, but I love hearing you say it."

"Then I'll say it again." She turned her head so she could look into his eyes. "I trust you with all my heart. No matter where we go, or what the future brings, I will always trust you."

Radek's expression softened into one of adoration and other, deeper emotions that filled her heart to overflowing. "To borrow a term from my Pyrosian friends – we are one."

The simple phrase resonated deep inside her soul. "Yes, we are."

With that, he settled into place behind her and guided his cock to her entrance. He entered her slowly, her body giving way to his with pleasure heightened by anticipation.

"Frost and Fire, you feel good," he exclaimed when he was completely sheathed inside her.

She rocked backward, grinding herself against him with a slow wiggle that sent a shiver through them both.

"Temptress," he muttered through clenched teeth. "You're teasing a dragon, remember?"

"I know. Bring it on, dragon man."

His hands tightened on her hips and his next words were accompanied by a rumbling growl. "You're sure?"

"Yes." She needed this. Needed him unleashed and wild. He withdrew fast and surged back into her without warning, slamming their bodies together with enough power she had to brace herself to stay upright. Desire poured through her like a molten river, setting fire to her blood as the mating fever swept her away.

Her fingers sank into the cushions, gripping them tightly as she rocked back against his thrusts. The sounds of their lovemaking filled the air, flesh on flesh, soft groans and wild cries. The scent of wildflowers and the forest blended with the smells of sex and sweat.

Radek moved over her, his chest pressed to her back as his thrusts grew harder and more uneven. He reached up to sweep her hair back from her neck, then his breath fanned her skin, and his teeth grazed the side of her throat.

She leaned her head to one side, baring her throat and he uttered a low rumbling growl of pleasure. He sank his fangs into her neck at the same time he reached around to press his wrist to her mouth. She bit him without even thinking about it, driven by instincts she didn't understand, but couldn't deny.

As her body exploded into orgasm she became aware that she wasn't alone. She could feel Radek's presence inside her as if his soul was flowing into hers, connecting them in the most intimate way imaginable. Time lost all meaning as she let herself drift in a sea of pleasure, her heart and soul so tangled up with Radek that she didn't know where he ended, and she began. This was her soulmate, the other half of her heart.

"*Ours.*" Her dragon's thoughts echoed her own.

She held onto their connection as long as she could, but eventually, the moment passed, and she found herself alone again. Not completely alone, though, there was a feeling of connection that hadn't been there before, as if Radek had left a piece of himself behind.

"I can still feel you," she whispered after they had parted and then tumbled into each others arms in a breathless tangle.

"And I can feel you." He touched a hand to his chest. "It's the final part of the mating bond. When I claimed you the first time, you were too close to death for us to experience this moment."

"But we can now? Do you think that's why I have fangs? Because I needed them for this?"

He wrapped his arms around her and cuddled her close. "I think your dragon knew what was needed and provided it. And yes, we can do this again, and each time we do, the bond between us will grow stronger." Radek chuckled and kissed her before adding. "You bit me, *sadina*. Now you're stuck with me forever."

She laughed with unfettered joy as he repeated her earlier words. "You better believe it, dragon man. Where you go, I follow."

CHAPTER SEVEN

Their idyllic escape ended far too soon. Radek could have happily spent months hidden away with Piper, but it wasn't possible. As the *rux* started to fade, Piper's concern about her family and friend grew stronger, compounded by guilt because she hadn't given them much thought in the last few days. The mating fever subsided to the point their dragons were calmer, and Piper had mastered the basics of flight well enough to make the journey back to the orbiting *Firebrand*. It was time to go home.

Attracting the Pyrosian's attention took time and a little effort. He covered the entire meadow outside their bower with a sheet of ice, while Piper used a spell he'd taught her to send countless orbs of blue and white light streaking into the sky. She'd gleefully skidded and danced over the ice, sending up the flares one after another. It took several hours for the *Firebrand's* scanners to locate them, but eventually, the anomalous appearance of the ice was noticed, and the flares confirmed their location. A shuttle had arrived not long after, and Piper had been elated to discover that not only were Aria and Haley safe and well, they were on board the *Firebrand*.

They were provided with new communicators and offered a ride back to the ship, but his dragon grew surly and possessive the moment a male Pyrosian guardsman approached Piper, a strong indication that it would be best if they waited a few more hours before returning.

He had stayed out of sight during Piper's brief conversation with her sibling, not wanting to intrude on their moment. He'd been close enough to listen, though, and what he heard made him envious. The sisters' love for each other was obvious in every word they spoke, even when Aria was chiding Piper for staying out of contact so long, despite Piper having already explained why it had been necessary. He couldn't remember the last time he'd spoken to any member of his family with such familiarity and affection. The youngest child by several decades, he had never been overly close with any of his siblings, but he hadn't realized how much distance had grown between them until he witnessed the bond between Piper and Aria. It made him see how solitary he'd become.

"What's wrong?" Piper asked the moment she'd returned to his side, the communicator inactive but still in her hand. "Are you dreading meeting my sister already? I promise, she's not usually that bad." She wrapped her arms around his waist in a comforting hug that warmed his heart and reminded him that he wasn't alone anymore.

"I look forward to meeting your family. Hearing you speak with your sister made me realize that my family haven't really been part of my life in too long. When we get home, I want to try and correct that, at least as much as they will allow it. We've drifted apart over the years. It's been ages since we were together for anything other than formal occasions that required us all to be present."

She looked up at him, lips pursed in thought. "It sounds like your family is missing their center. The one who brings everyone together and keeps the family bonds strong. After our mother died, there wasn't anyone left to keep our family together, either. I have cousins I haven't seen since her funeral."

He held her close and buried his face in her hair. "I know you are *my* center, *sadina*. You give me strength."

Piper uttered a contented sigh and leaned into him. "I like that. I'll be your center, and you can be my rock. The one I lean against when things get stormy."

"Yes." There were challenges ahead, but he had faith they would weather it together. Once his mother finally accepted the truth, his family would work alongside him to bring the temples back into line. There were priests who would fight to keep their power, but that was a battle he was prepared to fight.

PIPER FELT a pang of loss as she watched Radek dismiss the spell that had created their home for the past few days. In the blink of an eye, the ice melted away into nothingness. He spoke a few more words, and grass and plants that had been crushed beneath the weight of the building sprang back to life again. It was as if they'd never been there at all.

Radek leaned down and plucked a sprig of a purple and white wildflower. "We'll come back someday. I don't know how, or when, but this will not be the last time we see this place."

He spoke a few words under his breath, and the flower was suddenly encased in a crystalline pyramid which he offered to her with a smile. "Now we have something to remind us of our time here. A *mila* for my *mila*."

"I love it." She took it from him, then realized she had nowhere to put it. "How am I getting it to the ship, though? Do dragons have pockets I'm not aware of?"

"Actually, we do. Sort of. Anything you hold in your hands will transform with you."

"Handy. That means I'll never have to go without my lip balm."

He gave her a bemused look. "We used to carry our weapons and other necessary items that way, but yes, you can bring your lip balm, *mila*."

"Mock my lip balm addiction at your peril, dragon man. You know, I'm going to need a new nickname for you. It occurred to me that once we get to your world, your current moniker is going to apply to every male on the planet."

"I am your *sodono*, your mate."

"Mhmm. Accurate, but not very descriptive. What's the word in your language for a prince with a great ass?" she asked.

He arched a brow and smirked. "Radek."

She stuck her tongue out at him. "Fine. I'll pick a name for you once I've learned your language. You're sure this cognitive augmentation thing-y will work for me? We don't have time for me to learn Romaki the old-fashioned way."

"It's how I learned your language, and it's how the Pyrosian's plan on teaching the newly matched human females their language, culture, and history. I am confident they can make the adjustments needed to provide you with all you need to know."

"Good. I won't be much use to anyone if I can't understand what's being said."

He drew her into his arms and held her close, but even though she couldn't see his face, there was a hint of laughter in his next words. "I suspect you'd find a way to make your feelings known no matter what."

"You know I would."

He kissed the top of her head. "Are you ready?"

She gripped his gift in her hand and nodded. "I'm ready."

For safety's sake, Radek cast the spells required for their flight back to the *Firebrand*. She'd mastered a few basic skills, like conjuring a glass of water or the orbs of light she'd shot into the sky earlier. The most advanced thing she'd managed was to summon a change of clothing for herself and while she was getting pretty good at it, she wasn't going to risk her life by attempting something as complex as the magic needed to let them move and breathe once they left Earth's atmosphere.

There was a tingle that started at the top of her head, flowing over her body until it reached her toes. After that, they moved away from each other and transformed. For a moment they stared at each other, and she wondered again at how fantastically strange her life had gotten since she had first set eyes on Radek.

She roared her joy to the sky, unfurled her wings and took to the air with as much grace as she could master. Radek followed a moment later, and the two of them started to climb into the dazzling blue summer sky.

A shuttlecraft joined them as they reached the outer atmosphere, escorting them as they crossed into the icy darkness of true space. *"Aren't we supposed to be weightless?"* She asked Radek.

"Magic trumps physics," he replied.

"You're going to break the brains of an awful lot of human scientists when they discover magic is real. Please tell me I get to be there when you break the news to them."

"When the time comes, I expect we'll both be there to see it."

They flew in silence for a while. She could still feel their connection and it helped keep her calm and centred as they flew through the vacuum of space. Even with the protective spells in place she could feel the cold seep into her bones. There was no sound out here, and while she continued to flap her wings, she couldn't feel the wind anymore. It was an unsettling sensation, but the view more than made up for it. They were far enough away now that the blue edge of the planet was highlighted against the inky blackness while clouds the size of countries whirled and danced over the surface.

"We are coming back someday, right?" she asked, feeling her first moment of uncertainty at the idea of leaving everything she'd ever known.

"We will be back. I give you my word." He paused a moment, then added, *"If you look to your left you'll be able to see the* Firebrand. *Not much farther, now."*

She tore her eyes away from Earth to look in the direction he'd indicated and got her first look at a starship. It was everything she'd imagined, sleek and gleaming in the reflected light of the sun, its hull a stark white that shone like a beacon in the darkness. Somewhere on that ship her sister was waiting for her, and so was her future.

TIME FLEW FASTER than the *Firebrand* on the journey home, and before Piper knew it, it was time for her to go. It was harder to say goodbye to Aria and Melody than she expected. After working so long toward the goal of striking out on her own, when the moment finally came, Piper cried as much as her sister. "We'll talk every day. I promise."

Aria hugged her so tight Piper could barely breathe. "It's not going to be the same. I'm going to miss you so much. No one else knows how to make banana pancakes the way you do. And who is going to help put Melody to sleep when she's fussy?"

"Tarjen will help. Melody adores him, and he's totally smitten with both of you." Tarjen was devoted, steadfast, and so in love with Aria and Melody, it made her smile every time she saw them all together. In the weeks since they'd left Earth behind, she'd gotten to know Tarjen and Torel well enough to be certain they would take good care of the people she cared about.

"That's not the point. Why did you have to go and fall in love with an alien from another planet?" Aria said.

Piper burst out laughing. "It must run in the family."

"Yeah, but you had to fall for a guy from a *different* planet! One that isn't all that keen on outsiders. What if they come after you with pitchforks or something?"

"Ri, they're not a mob from the Middle Ages."

"No, they're *dragons!*"

She hugged her sister and then stepped back and winked at her. "And so am I. I'll be fine, I promise."

Tarjen came over to them, cradling a cooing Melody in the crook of one arm. "It's time, *seska.*"

"I know." Aria sighed and then grabbed Piper in one last hug. "Take care of yourself…your Highness."

Before she left, Piper turned to her brother-in-law. "Take care of them for me, please. Oh, and I left you detailed instructions on how to make my banana pancakes. Not even Ri has the recipe. They're guaranteed to make my sister feel better about anything and everything."

He smiled down at her and gave her a gentle hug. "I will take care of them, now and forever more. Good luck, Highness. May the Gods watch over you both."

"They got me into this mess, they better not abandon me now."

"Bye, Piper. You're going to be amazing!" Haley called out.

Vadir appeared at the door of his ship and waved. "Time to go." Radek's friend, Vadir had offered to make the trip to Romak to deliver them home. They'd be there in less than a week. She couldn't wait to start her new life. If it was half as wonderful as Radek's descriptions, she was going to love it there.

CHAPTER EIGHT

RADEK CHECKED his attire one last time, making sure everything was perfect. The moment they stepped off the ship they would be scrutinized by everyone they encountered.

"If you don't stop fussing with those buttons, you're going to pop them right off." Piper took hold of his hands and held them in hers. "Tell me again that this is going to be fine, please?" She spoke in Romaki, as fluently as if she'd known the language for years instead of weeks.

"It *will* be fine. You have nothing to worry about. Just keep your head high and remember, you are a member of the royal family, and my mate."

"A mate none of them know about." She bit her lower lip. "I still think we should have told them about me ahead of time."

He squeezed her hands and smiled down at her. "We didn't tell them about you because I wanted you to be a surprise. You are the proof that I was right, and I want everyone to be there to see what a beautiful, amazing female the Gods gifted me with. You are my center, *sadina*."

She gave him a small but trusting smile. "And you are my rock, *sodono*."

"Good luck." Vadir stood in the door of the cockpit, looking as calm and collected as usual.

"Have fun storming the castle!" Lisa added from just behind him. They would hang back for a few minutes to make sure everything was going smoothly before joining them on the palace grounds.

Radek stepped up to the door and took Piper's hand in his. "Cas, please open the door."

"Door opening. It was a pleasure having you on board."

Pipers grip tighten around his fingers. "I love you."

It was the first time she'd said those words. It added another level of magnitude to this already special moment. "I love you, too." He squared his shoulders and walked into the winter sunshine with Piper at his side.

The grounds were crowded, full of curious onlookers and courtiers with a vested interest in seeing which way the winds of fortune blew today. It wasn't difficult to spot his family—they were waiting together beneath a pavilion, flanked by priests from both temples. Solun on the left, and Daga on the right. No one from his family moved or spoke, they simply watched his approach with carefully blank expressions.

He walked through the sea of faces without seeing any of them, eyes front, head up, the way he'd been trained to carry himself since he was a child. When he reached the pavilion where his parents were seated, he bowed low, and so did Piper, exactly the way they had rehearsed it. Then he stood and waited for his mother to speak. She took her time, and her gaze lingered on Piper a long while before she finally broke the silence.

"Welcome home, my son. I am happy to have you back with us. Now, please give me one good reason why I should not have you thrown into prison for breaking the law, abandoning your duties, and leaving this world for the empty spaces far from the protection of the Gods."

Piper exhaled sharply, and her hand tightened around his, but her expression didn't change. His mother's frosty reception took him by surprise.

"I am pleased to be home." He turned to Piper. "I am even more pleased to be able to introduce you to my mate, Piper Frasier." He paused for the barest second before adding, "of the planet Earth."

There was a collective gasp as everyone within earshot reacted to his announcement, and the noise expanded as those who had heard spread the news to their neighbours. Within a few seconds, there was a general clamour and the crowd surged in closer as everyone tried to get a better look at Piper. She ignored them, keeping her head up and her eyes locked on him. She looked every part a princess, garbed in a dress of deep blue, her cloak the purest shade of silver. He had taught her an incantation that allowed her to change her hair colour at will. Today it was the same brilliant blue it had been the first day he'd seen her.

"That's not possible!" a priest of Solun declared. Radek recognized him. Tredon. He was the head of their order in all but name. An ambitious male with a love for power far greater than his love for the God he professed to speak for.

"Are you calling my son, the youngest-born prince of Genesa Makyrn, ruler of the Snow Dragon Clan, a liar?" There was ice in his mother's words.

Tredon's mouth fell open, his eyes wide with alarm. "I am saying that your son must be…mistaken. The Gods would not condone a mating between a Romaki and a being from another species. Perhaps this is his punishment. In his absence, the prince has become delusional."

"Is that true, Radek? Are you delusional?"

His mother might not be happy with him, but at least she was giving him an opportunity to defend himself. "No, Mother. I am not delusional. Nor have I been punished by the Gods for leaving this world. I have traversed the galaxy and flown the skies of a distant world. A world that has legends about dragons. About us. I have read legends about our kind and seen works of art that prove that we were once visitors on that planet."

"Can your female confirm this?" his mother asked. He didn't like the fact she had not referred to Piper as his mate, or even by name.

Piper nodded, stepped forward, and answered for herself in perfect Romaki. "It's true, Highness. There are legends about dragons on my world. Ancient stories, hundreds of years old."

"Heresy!" Tredon hissed.

"Truth," Piper retorted. "The only one lying here today is you. You know there have been other matings between Romaki and members of other species. I am not the first, nor will I be the last."

Radek was struck by a dizzying mix of pride and panic as Piper stood up to the priest. How had things gotten so far out of hand? He had expected resistance, but nothing like this.

The situation escalated again when Tredon puffed out his chest, raised his voice and pointed straight at Piper. "You are an outsider! You have no right to speak to me that way. Be silent!"

Radek stepped forward but stopped when his mother raised her hand in a brusque gesture. "You forget yourself, Priest of Solun. We are not in your temple, we are on the grounds of my home. I rule here, and I will determine who speaks, and when."

The crowd went silent, and everyone's gaze bounced from his mother to the chastised priest, and then to Piper. They knew something momentous was happening, but it was too soon to tell what shape it would take. Honestly, he didn't know, either. He had expected there to be some mutterings over his decision to leave Romak, but no priest should feel empowered enough to speak to any member of the royal family the way Tredon had. If he went after Piper again, Radek would end him, consequences be damned.

"It would seem that despite your warnings, my son has not been punished by the Gods. I'd say this requires further investigation, don't you agree?" Genesa asked in a voice that brooked no argument.

"We would like to investigate this further, Highness," said one of the high-ranking priestesses from the temple of Daga.

"Of…of course. If that is your wish, Highness," Tredon finally muttered without meeting anyone's gaze.

"Excellent. Since we are all in agreement. I suggest we adjourn inside to welcome my son and his…mate, home properly." His mother rose to her feet, and everyone started to move towards the palace.

Piper tugged on his hand. "You didn't tell me it would be like this."

"I didn't think it would be. Things should go better once we've had a chance to explain everything in detail. You're my mate. They have to accept what that means."

She gave a tiny shake of her head and pursed her lips. "And if they don't? Your own mother threatened to throw you in prison! Maybe we should turn around and hitch a ride back to Pyros with Vadir and Lisa."

"We can't go, *sadina*. There's too much at stake. This is the fight we came here for, remember?"

"I didn't expect to be fighting your own family. Even when Aria and I were at each other's throats it was never like this. We were still *family*. None of yours even smiled in greeting. They're all stone-faced and grim. No wonder you left this place."

"I left because I had to." He looked up at the palace, to the balcony he'd been standing on the night Vadir had made his offer. So much had changed since that moment. Now, he just had to make his family listen to him long enough to accept he was right.

Piper stayed at Radek's side and never once let go of his hand. The crush of people was thick enough that if they were parted she wasn't sure she'd be able to get back to him. Everyone was staring at her, most with curiosity, but some with open hostility. She didn't understand. Radek had warned her there would be those who were uneasy around off-worlders, but she was mated to Radek. According to their own beliefs, she'd been chosen by their Gods as his mate, so why were they being so hostile?

Piper looked ahead of her and caught a glimpse of Genesa, Radek's mother. Her back was stiff as she moved through the crowd, and the press of bodies parted in front of her and her guards like she was Moses crossing the Red Sea. Piper had heard enough stories from Radek to know that Genesa wasn't a gentle, nurturing sort of woman, but she hadn't been prepared to come face to face with the living definition of an ice queen.

Once inside, Radek escorted her to a quiet corner.

There were palace employees everywhere, taking the guests' cloaks and jackets, serving trays of drinks and delicacies, and subtly orchestrating the flow of beings so that some were moved closer to the royal family, and others found themselves being politely deflected to other parts of the room. It was quite the room, too. The entire vaulted ceiling was painted with a mural depicting blue and red dragons soaring in a dark blue sky while the walls had multiple alcoves that accommodated statues of both people and dragons.

A server approached with a tray of steaming drinks, and Radek let go of her hand to select two drinks. "It's *korta*," he told her as he handed her one of the mugs.

"Got anything stronger?" She murmured, but she accepted the drink, cradling the warm metal in her hands."

"Tempting, but given how things are unfolding, it might be best if we stay sober and alert."

She agreed with his logic, even if she would have loved a shot of liquid courage to help her deal with everything.

Another staff member approached. "Highness, your father has requested a brief meeting while your mother is attending to matters of court."

"Of course." He held out his hand to Piper, but the man cleared his throat. "Apologies, Highness. Your father specified this was to be a *private* meeting."

Radek's jaw set in a stubborn line. "I am not leaving my mate."

"We'll stay with her." Vadir appeared beside Radek.

"You bet we will. Us Earth girls are going to stick together, right Piper?" Lisa asked. She already had a drink in her hand and looked completely at ease.

"Don't be long." She flashed Radek what she hoped was a confident smile. If his father wanted to talk to him, it was likely important. While it stung that she hadn't been included in the invitation, she was starting to realize the idea to surprise everyone with her arrival might not have been the best approach.

Radek moved in and kissed her with enough heat to make her toes tingle. "I'll be back as soon as I can. I promise."

"You better be."

He nodded, then gestured to the man to lead him to his father.

The moment he left, her anxiety started to climb. She had expected him to stay with her during these first moments. As much as she liked Vadir and Lisa, they weren't Radek.

"You doing okay?" Lisa asked in English.

"All things considered? Yeah, I guess so," Piper answered in the same language, ensuring that even if they were overheard no one would know what they were saying.

Lisa snorted. "All things considered, your new family kinda sucks. And what was with that priest? I thought Radek was going to tear his head off for a second there."

"If he'd said another word, I think he might have." At least his mother had put a stop to that nonsense.

Vadir started to say something, then raised his head to look at something over her shoulder and groaned. "Wonderful. Savta is heading this way. You ready to play meet the ex?"

"Ex? What ex? Who the hell is Savta?"

Vadir blanched. "Radek didn't mention her?"

"No."

"Wish I had time to explain, but uh, good luck and don't listen to a thing that comes out of her mouth, okay?"

"Vadir! I didn't realize you'd be returning to us so soon." Savta almost purred her greeting, setting Piper's teeth on edge before she even got a glimpse of this woman who was apparently Radek's ex…something.

She nearly snapped her fangs off when she saw Savta for the first time. The woman was the epitome of elegance. Her dress was a shimmering fall of metallic blue fabric that clung to every perfect curve of her body. Her hair was swept up in an elaborate series of braids, framing a face so lovely she should probably be classified as a work of art.

"Savta! Always a delight to see you at these functions." Lisa handed her drink to her mate and stepped in front of Savta just as the new arrival laid her hand on Vadir's shoulder. She threw her arms around Savta's neck and hugged her so hard the other woman uttered an alarmed little squawk. The moment Lisa released her, Savta hurriedly moved away from them both. Once she could breathe again, she ran her gaze over Lisa's outfit, a bright red dress with pink and white polka dots and matching boots. "I always enjoy your visits, Lisa. You have such an interesting interpretation of what's in fashion."

And the claws are out already. Awesome.

Lisa merely smiled and cozied into Vadir's side. "Thank you. Polka dots are all the rage on Pyros right now. I'm sure the trend will make its way to Romak, eventually."

Savta's lips thinned slightly, and instead of responding, she turned to Piper. "Forgive me for not waiting for a proper introduction, but I was so curious to meet the female Radek claims is his mate I had to come over. I am Savta Brektar, Radek's consort."

For a second, Piper couldn't breathe, and a red-hot jolt of jealousy hit, followed by a low rumbling growl deep inside her head. Her dragon didn't like the idea of sharing Radek's affection any more than she did.

She took all that jealousy and hurt and channelled it into something she could use – righteous anger. "I'm Radek's mate, Piper Anderson. I'll forgive your curiosity if you forgive mine. How long were you and Radek together? I can't imagine it was very long, since he never mentioned you to me."

Savta's silver eyes narrowed, and Piper knew she'd scored a direct hit. "How interesting. We've known each other since we were children. I can't imagine why he wouldn't tell you about me. After all, I'm the female his mother chose for him."

"And I am the female the *Gods* chose for him." She lowered her voice to conspirator's whisper. "To be honest, we didn't do a lot of talking after we met. The effects of the *rux* are so intense, and they lasted for days and days. Who wants to talk about old flames at a time like that?"

"The *rux*? But…you're not Romaki."

"I wasn't, no." She flashed her fangs and allowed her dragon one small growl. "But I am now."

"The queen has been so distraught over all this. First Radek's rash decision to defy her and the Gods, and now…" Savta looked down her nose at Piper. "Now he has returned with you."

"The Gods never wanted the Romaki to stay locked away on this one little world. If they had, they would have punished Radek instead of rewarding him."

"Are you a reward, though?" Savta gave her a cruel little smile. "The way I see it, the prince has been punished. He could have done so much better for himself."

Piper's temper flared. "He clearly didn't think you were much of a prize. He left the planet and travelled across the galaxy to get away from you. Whatever you were to him, I'm here now, and Radek is mine."

Her dragon added a warning growl to her final words, and Savta wisely chose to walk away instead of saying another word. Her expression was one of haughty disdain as she turned her back on Piper and left, with barely a nod to Vadir and Lisa on her way by.

Piper held herself together until she was certain the bitch was out of earshot, then exhaled hard. "Fuck! What the hell did Radek see in that woman?"

Lisa took the mug of *korta* out of Piper's hand and replaced it with a flute of something she hoped was booze. "I have no idea, but I don't think she'll be messing with you again any time soon. I really do not like that woman. Every time she sees Vadir she gets all touchy-feely. One of these days I'm going to braid her fingers together."

"No, you won't, because you know that I have no interest in her. You're the only female I want." Vadir put his arm around Lisa, then looked over at Piper. "And you are my new favourite person. Nice job handling Savta."

Before she could say anything more, Radek rushed back to her. "Are you alright, *mila*?"

"Not even close. When were you going to mention the fact you had a consort waiting for you back home?"

He winced. "She isn't my consort. Well, not officially."

"Not officially?" she raised her voice as much as she dared and moved away from him.

"I knew I shouldn't have left you alone."

"Not the point right now. Any other surprises for me today? Lovers I need to meet? Ancient laws I broke just by daring to exist?"

When he sighed instead of answering her right away, she knew there was more bad news coming. "Tomorrow morning, you and I are to meet with my mother and the rest of my family in private. There are questions that need to be answered."

"They're putting us on trial?"

"No, *sadina*. They want to understand what has happened."

"Frankly, so do I. This isn't what you promised me. I came here to show your people a new future, and they're so frightened of what that means they're treating me like I'm the enemy." She drained the glass Lisa had handed her and then shoved it at Radek. "I don't think anyone will miss me if I leave this party early. In fact, I'm sure they'll be quite happy when I'm gone. I'm out of here."

"You don't even know where you're going." He reached for her, but she wouldn't let him touch her. She couldn't. She was too angry and confused. She'd reached her breaking point.

"Then find me someone who does to help me."

"*Sadina…*"

She held up a hand, almost imploring him to stop talking. "No. I can't talk to you right now. I just can't."

Vadir cleared his throat. "We can show her to your rooms, Highness. I know the way."

Looking deflated now, Radek nodded. "I will stay here for the next hour or so. If anyone asks, the excitement of the day taxed you, and you went to our rooms for some rest."

"Sure, that works." She looked over at Lisa. "Get me out of here before I snap and start eating people. I already know which one I'm starting with."

Lisa laughed. "You got it. And you don't want to eat that bitch. She'd be so bitter she'd pucker your face forever."

Piper didn't look back at Radek until they were across the room. He was still standing in the corner, watching her go with sad silver eyes. Her dragon rumbled inside her head, but Piper ignored her. It's not like she was leaving him forever. Hell, they were mated. She was so tightly connected to him she couldn't leave him if she tried.

CHAPTER NINE

VADIR WALKED AHEAD OF THEM, taking her through the twists and turns of the palace without hesitation. She had no idea where they were, or how he was finding his way. To her, it all looked the same, and she'd need a map and a compass to find her way around. Lisa walked with her, keeping her company without saying a word. It was exactly what she needed. When they reached the door of what turned out to be Radek's rooms, Vadir opened it and stepped aside. "Welcome home."

It struck her that he was the first person to say that since she'd gotten here. She stepped inside, then turned to say, "Thanks. I'm not sure this is home, though. Right now, I'm not sure about anything."

Lisa and Vadir shared a look. "Do you want to be alone right now, or would you like me to stay with you for a bit?" Lisa asked.

Her first instinct was to tell them to go, but when

she thought about it, she changed her mind. "Would you mind staying? If you go, I'll officially have run out of people I know on this planet."

"Of course I'll stay." Lisa nodded to Vadir, who waited until they were both inside and then closed the door, leaving them alone. Everything in the room was either dark blue or black. The rugs, the furnishings—even the paintings were abstracts done in similar colours. The walls were pale grey, the floors polished grey stone, and every table was a gleaming slab of black or blue crystal. There were doors leading off to other rooms, but she didn't go exploring, yet.

Lisa came over and hugged her. "I'm something of an expert at having your life turned upside down by a sexy alien with lousy communication skills. If you want to talk, I'm here. If you'd rather do some primal screaming, I'm down for that, too."

"I could use a drink and a friend to talk to." Piper looked around the room. "And maybe we can plan some serious redecorating before you and Vadir leave. I am not living in the Romaki version of bachelor paradise."

"Whatever you need, Vadir can get. After the lousy way he warned you about Savta, he owes you that much. Honestly, I think that female unsettles him, and that's saying something."

Lisa settled herself onto one of the dark navy couches that lined the walls of what was some sort of sitting area, while Piper went searching for something to drink.

She found a couple of bottles sitting on a side table, and a quick sniff of the contents confirmed one of them was alcoholic, and one was some kind of fruit juice. It was even chilled. There weren't any glasses around, but she'd mastered enough magic to conjure her own. It took a moment to calm herself enough to focus on the words, but she managed to create two simple glasses and pour them each a drink. Fruit juice for Lisa, because she was pregnant.

"It's so amazing how you can do that. You just made these glasses appear!"

"I know. I'm still getting used to the idea I can use magic." Piper sat down beside Lisa and sank into the cushions with a sigh. "I guess that's part of the reason I'm so surprised everyone is questioning this. Before I met Radek, magic wasn't real. How can they doubt this is real? I'm a freaking dragon, for Gods' sake."

Lisa sipped her juice. "They might be aliens, but they still share some traits with humans. I've met several races of aliens so far, and you'd be amazed how many things we all have in common. They can be petty, greedy, and cruel just as easily as they can be kind, or helpful, or loving."

"You forgot really bad at communicating."

"You think Radek's bad? Vadir didn't even tell me he was an alien until he teleported me onto his ship and tried to fly away with me. Then he went and made all sorts of plans for what our life was going to be like, only he never asked me what I wanted."

"He didn't tell you he wasn't human?" Piper took a

big swig of her drink, ignoring the burn and the way it made her eyes water. "Okay, that's a pretty big oversight. How did you two get past it?"

"Well, I might have punched him and crashed his ship. After that, I kind of had to drag him to the medical bay to get him fixed up. Then we had crazy wild sex, and then a fight, and then more sex, and here we are."

"You punched him, and he mated you anyway? And now you don't fight anymore?"

Lisa burst out laughing. "Of course we fight. And then we have wild make-up sex and the cycle begins again. I love him, but he makes me crazy sometimes. And of course, he's my mate. Once the Spark happened, that part was inevitable. That doesn't make it easy, though." She lit up. "You know who we need to be part of this conversation? Your sister. She and Tarjen didn't exactly have the galaxy's most perfect courtship, either."

"It sure seemed pretty perfect to me." Piper was conflicted about talking to Aria. On the one hand, she missed her sister and could use the moral support. On the other hand, Aria was probably going to overreact and treat her like she was a kid again, complete with a litany of I told you sos.

"No one's relationship is perfect. I remember the moment she stormed out of Tarjen's room with Melody in her arms and no idea where she was going. We grabbed her and sent our mates over to help Tarjen figure out where he'd gone wrong."

"She didn't tell me that."

"She probably didn't want to admit it to her little sister." Lisa set a small cube down on the table in front of them. "Cas, you there?"

"I am able to hear you, yes. But I am not there with you. I cannot leave the ship, remember?"

Lisa rolled her eyes at the AI that ran Vadir's ship. "Don't be literal, Cas. You know I hate that. Can you contact Aria on Pyros and let her know her sister would like to speak with her?"

"Relaying the message, now."

"Where's the disconnect button on this thing? If Ri starts lecturing me on my lack of judgement and reckless ways, I'm hanging up on her," she warned Lisa.

"Or you could tell her that's not helpful and redirect the conversation," Lisa replied.

"Oh sure, be logical." Piper took several generous sips of her drink while they waited. It wasn't long. The device beeped and the air above it started to shimmer. A few seconds later, her sister's head and shoulders appeared, floating in midair.

"I didn't expect to hear from you so soon after landing. Are you okay? How did it go?" Aria asked.

Piper waved. "Hi, Sis. It went… not great, actually. Radek's mom is hardcore, the priests are pissed and want to investigate my claims, and uh, Radek might have forgotten to mention that part of the reason he left was because he was about to be forced to take a consort. I met her, she's a total bitch."

"So you're on your way back to Pyros? Tell me you're safe on Vadir's ship and coming here."

"No, I'm in Radek's quarters with Lisa, having a drink while I process this shit-storm."

"What's to process? You did what you always do and jumped in without thinking things through. Now, you need to get out of there. You said the priests want to investigate? That sounds bad. You're not safe."

"I'm fine, Ri. I'm just hurt and confused. You telling me this is all a mistake and I need to bail is not helping me feel better. I'm mated, remember? Just like you and Tarjen."

Aria sighed. "Sorry. Old habits die hard."

"I know, but really, can't we kill that one already?" Frustration at everything going on put an edge to her words. "When are you going to finally accept that I'm an adult with a life of my own?"

"I'm trying." Aria pinched the bridge of her nose and was quiet for a moment. "Can I call a do-over?"

Piper had to laugh. Their mother had invented the do-over rule as a way of letting her re-set conversations and arguments that had gotten out of hand. It was a bit silly, but it worked. "Yeah, you can."

Aria counted to three, then started again. "Hi, Piper. I didn't expect to hear from you so soon after landing. Are you okay? How did it go?"

"Not great. I could really use some advice from my big sister right now."

Aria smiled. "I'm here. Tell me what happened?"

Piper took a deep breath and started talking, telling

her sister everything from the moment they walked off the ship until she and Lisa had sat down. By the time she was done, she felt a little better. Like the ground had settled under her feet again.

"You should have seen her deal with Savta. It was a thing of beauty, Aria. You would have been proud of your little sister," Lisa said.

Aria's smile broadened. "I am proud of her. I always have been. You know that, right, Piper?"

There was a lump in Piper's throat as she nodded. "It's still nice to hear it sometimes."

"I guess you and I are a work in progress. Probably always will be. Most relationships are like that. Tarjen and I are working on us, too. I can read his thoughts and his feelings and there are still times he annoys the hell out of me."

"Tell me about it," Lisa chimed in.

"At least you have some idea what your mates are thinking. I have no clue what's going through Radek's head most of the time. He made this all sound like it was going to be an adventure, but this… Savta flat out said I must be Radek's punishment from the Gods. These people hate me!"

"No, Savta hates you. Everyone else is just figuring out who you are and what it means that you're here."

"She wasn't the only one looking at me like they'd like to see me dead and buried, and not necessarily in that order."

"Were they all women?" Aria asked.

Piper thought back. "Women and priests."

"There's your answer," Aria said. "Radek is hot by the standards of any species. He was also rich, unmated, and a member of royalty. I bet there were any number of females hoping to catch his interest. This consort thing, it only lasts until one of the pair finds their mates, right? It must, because once one of them was mated, they wouldn't want anyone else. That's how it works with the Pyrosians, anyway."

"It's the same for the Romaki." Aria made a good point. Whatever there might have been between Radek and Savta, it ended the moment Radek claimed her as his mate.

"It's nice to know that whatever else we might face, at least our men will never cheat on us," Aria said.

"Amen," Lisa agreed, then turned to Piper. "So, now that you're calmer, what do you want to do? Vadir and I can whisk you out of here, with or without Radek, or you can stay and do what you can."

"I...I don't know. This isn't what I signed up for."

"Life rarely works that way." Aria pointed to herself, then Lisa, then Piper. "I'm sure none of us thought we'd be mated to guys from another planet, living on the other side of the galaxy from Earth and everyone we know. The question is, what is it you want? I've known you your whole life, Pi. You're unstoppable when you're going after something you really want. You just need to decide what that is."

"Lisa, you're psychic. Any chance you can drop me a hint as to what comes next?" she asked.

Lisa laughed. "Nope. You need to make this choice

on your own. I knew that if Radek went to Earth, his life would change. I didn't tell him that, though. Vadir made him an offer, but he had to make the decision to leave Romak. Now it's your turn to make a choice."

"Whatever you decide, you know I'll be there for you," Aria added.

"I know. I love you, too, sis, and thanks for helping me work through this. If you ever need me, you know I'm there for you, too."

"Next time Tarjen tries to plan Melody's entire life from now until the day she dies, I'll call you and you can talk me down. Code word will be wine time."

"Deal," Piper said.

"And now I'm missing my friends. I really need to call them. Maybe we'll set up a wine time, too. You guys are invited, of course." Lisa rose from the couch and touched her temple. "You going to be okay if I go? Vadir just let me know that Savta is circling him like a shark, and he's hoping I'm coming back down before she does something stupid.

"Oh, and he says Radek is out in the garden pacing in circles and not talking to anyone. Want me to send him up once I find him?"

"Yes," her dragon murmured from the back of her mind.

"Forgiven him already?"

"Miss him."

So did she. It was the longest they'd been apart since they'd met. "Send him up. We need to talk about what happened, and what happens next."

"I'm going to go, too. Melody will be up from her nap any second." Aria waved. "Talk later and let me know how things are going, okay?"

"I will." The call disconnected, Lisa gathered up her gizmo, and a few minutes later Piper was alone. She wandered over to the heavy curtains that covered what had to be an outer wall and pulled them back to discover a set of glass doors that led to a massive balcony with a breathtaking view of the capital. The sun was setting, but there was still a little time left before night fell. She wanted to see the city. Apart from a brief look as they'd flown in, she hadn't seen any of it yet. She stepped outside and let the cold winter air clear her mind as she looked out over her new home. If she stayed. If they let her stay. She mulled over everything that had happened, and all that Lisa and her sister had said. She was still thinking when she heard the door open.

"*Sadina?*" Radek called.

"Out here," she replied without turning around.

His booted footsteps rang out on the stone floor, and the next thing she knew she was engulfed in a bear hug from behind and lifted off her feet. "I missed you. I'm sorry. If you wish to leave, we'll go. Now. I've already spoken to Vadir."

"I missed you, too." She wrapped her arms around his waist and turned her head as much as she could. "Savta is a serious bitch."

He nuzzled her cheek tenderly, still holding her tight. "Which is why I refused to have anything to do with her. The night I left, I told her that even if my mother ordered me to take her as my consort, I'd never share her bed."

"Never? So you two weren't…"

"Never." He moved his lips in a slow line back to her ear. "Not even when I was a foolish, randy youth did I find her at all desirable. She may be lovely on the outside, but there's so much ugliness inside her it repels me."

"Good answer."

"It's the truth. I swear to you by Solun's hoary beard, there has never been anything between us. She is a vile, venomous female who was only interested in me because of who my parents are."

"And yet, that's the female your mother wanted for you."

His next words were tinged with sadness. "My mother chose her for political reasons, which is the motivation behind most of these kinds of arrangements. I'm sure she was aware of my feelings about Savta, though. She probably thought that forcing me to accept her as consort would make me reconsider my stubborn refusal to bow to the temple's wisdom. She believed the priests, who insisted that once I stopped arguing with their laws, I would find my mate."

"I'm sorry she did that to you. I wouldn't wish that harpy on my worst enemy. Still, you should have said something. All I got was a three-second warning from Vadir that your ex was headed my way, and then she was in my face, telling me how she was the female your mother had chosen for you and that I am clearly your punishment for defying the Gods."

He went still for a long moment, and when he moved again, it was to crush her to his chest. "She said what?"

"That I was your punishment. You could have done so much better."

He growled, the low rumble rising from his chest and rolling through her. "I will have her banned from the palace. She has been testing the limits of propriety for some time. This is the final straw."

"But she has your mother's favour. I think it's pretty obvious who she's going to side with if she has to choose between Savta and her new daughter-in-law. Your mother hates me."

Radek finally set her down. "Actually, I think she was impressed by you. If she wasn't she wouldn't have stopped Tredon the way she did."

She turned toward him. "Could have fooled me."

"My mother is not an easy woman to know, but I've been on her bad side often enough to tell when she is truly angry. The only real anger she showed today was toward Tredon."

"Well, yeah. He was a jerk, and he forgot his place."

He shook his head. "It's been a long time since anyone reminded him what his place is, including my mother. Something changed while I was gone. My father hinted at it, but we couldn't speak openly."

"So that's what he wanted to talk to you about?

Why wasn't I allowed to be part of that conversation, then?"

"Because one of the things he wanted to discuss was you."

Icy claws of dread took hold of her heart. "What did he say? Are they going to make me leave? Is this why you talked to Vadir? Are they going to try and say we're not mated?"

He pulled her into his arms and crushed her to him again. It wasn't the easiest way to have a serious conversation, but she didn't care. "No, *mila*. He was concerned for you. For us, actually. Which was a nice change. It was a cryptic conversation, but he made it clear that he and my mother will not allow the priests to push their agenda too far. They are on our side."

"You sure about that? She did threaten to toss you in a cell as I recall."

"She did. But if she meant that to happen, she would have ordered it done the moment we left the ship."

"If they're on our side, why would we leave?"

Radek looked down at her with affection. "Because this is not going to be as easy as I thought. Because I didn't think to forewarn you about Savta. Because you deserve better than how you were treated today. If you want to go, then we'll leave."

"But your dreams…"

"Are not more important than your happiness."

"Thank you." She wrapped her arms around his waist and hugged him. "But we're not going anywhere. Not yet, anyway. I came here because I believed you when you said this was the Gods' will. I still believe that. So, now we have to figure out a way to convince the rest of your people that you're right and the priests are wrong."

He bowed his head over hers, pressing their foreheads together as he looked into her eyes. "You never cease to amaze me."

"I'm pretty amazing, I know. You should have heard me lay into Savta. Lisa said it was a thing of beauty."

"I'm sure it was. I am also sure you will be the one to get the last word because she will never be permitted near you again."

"Have I mentioned that I like it when you get all growly and protective?"

"You haven't, lately."

"Well, I do. And now we're in this hornet's nest, I'm going to like it even more. I wanted to see your homeworld and find a way to make it my home." She pointed to the city beyond the palace walls. "I'm not sure when I'm going to get to see it."

"How about now?"

"Now? There's a party going on downstairs, and you're supposed to be the guest of honour, remember? They might notice if we walk out the front door."

He grinned. "Who said anything about walking? We're dragons, *sadina*. If you want to see the city, then we'll do it, from the air."

"We can do that?"

He kissed the tip of her nose and then released her, stepping back to gesture to the wide-open area of the balcony. "Why do you think this space is so large? It's big enough to accommodate a dragon, or two."

"If you think it's a good idea…" She wanted to go, but the idea of changing forms and flying off so publicly was strange to her.

"The priests are already trying to cast doubts about our mating, claiming that you are not a Romaki. I can think of no better way to prove them wrong." He moved to the far side of the balcony and grinned again. "Come fly with me, my mate."

With that, he transformed. Before she had time to do more than blink, he was in the air, looking back at her as he rose. She followed him a few seconds later, and together they flew into the winter twilight.

If this was what life would be like here, maybe she'd learn to love it, after all.

CHAPTER TEN

THE PALACE WAS as quiet as it ever got when Radek took Piper by the hand and led her to the family dining room. He couldn't remember the last time they'd all been there together. It had to be years, if not decades since his entire family had gathered there to share a meal. It was smaller and far less ornate than the public rooms, and even more importantly, it was protected by a security system that ensured that no one would be able to gain entry or listen to what was said once the doors were closed. Not even the waitstaff would be allowed to stay inside. Because of this, breakfast would be a buffet-style affair.

The last of the staff were leaving just as they entered, and the tantalizing scents of the morning meal hit him the moment they arrived. Piper's stomach rumbled, and he knew exactly how she felt.

"Can we help ourselves, or do we wait for your parents to arrive?" she asked.

"Help ourselves. See? My siblings have already started."

She gave him a worried look. "So, we're late? If we are, I'm blaming you and your theory that it would be faster if we showered together."

One of his sisters caught Piper's comment and snickered, then stopped to speak with them. "My Cyros likes to try that one on me, too. I am Syna. You must be Piper. Welcome to the family."

Piper gave her a warm smile. "Thank you. You're the first one to say that."

Syna nodded. "I figured. The others are still trying to figure out what your arrival means, and how they can best benefit from it. Me, I'm just looking forward to the fireworks." She leaned in and whispered. "I heard you met Savta and put her in her place. That's when I knew I was going to like you."

Syna was his closest sibling by age, but she had found her mate young and left the palace for her new life in the court of the Fire Dragon Clan while Radek was still a boy. He had always liked her, but time and distance had allowed them to drift apart. He was grateful that she was still as kind and wild as he remembered. "It's good to see you, Syna." He reached out and gave her a light, one-armed hugged.

"You, too." She hugged him back with unexpected strength. "I've missed you, little brother."

"I've missed you, too. I've been gone a long time, but I'm back now."

"Good." Syna lowered her voice again. "We need

you and your mate. You'll see what I mean once Mother gets here. Until then, eat up. We're all going to need our strength."

With that, she wandered off again, leaving him wondering what Syna knew that he didn't.

Piper leaned into his side and murmured, "Well, that was cryptic and a little ominous. I'm glad at least one member of your family is happy to meet me, though. She is officially my favourite now."

"Mine, too."

He led her over to the buffet and helped her identify the various foods, she was as brave and curious as always, taking a little bit of everything new so she could try them. Apart from Syna, no one had spoken more than a few words of greeting to either he or Piper.

They had only taken a few bites when a side door opened, and his parents joined them. For once, his mother wore her silver-white hair in a long, single braid with no crown or jewels, she wore a simple day dress, and his father was equally casual in his appearance. This was a rare day, indeed.

They all stood as his parents entered and stayed standing until they had gathered their breakfast and sat down at the far end of the table. Once Genesa was seated, she turned to Radek and spoke in a voice designed to carry. "Good morning everyone. And good morning Radek and Piper. You left before I could speak to you again last night." She raised one white brow. "I trust you enjoyed your flight?"

"Good morning, mother. Yes, we did enjoy

ourselves. I promised Piper I would show her the city, and it seemed the right time."

"During a party that was held in your honour?" Genesa asked.

"After my mate was accosted by one of the guests at that party and chose to leave rather than risk more unpleasantness, yes."

"Indeed." Was all his mother said.

She took a few bites of her meal, then looked at him again. "You could never do things the easy way, my child. Why is that?"

"I suspect it's because he takes after his mother," his father stated with a small smile.

Everyone stilled as they waited to see how she took that remark. No one even breathed until Genesa nodded slightly.

"Possibly," Genesa admitted. "What have you got to say for yourself? Do you have any idea how worried we've been, my son? You disappeared! Frankly, I was starting to wonder if Savta had managed to have you killed and hidden the body."

"Savta? The female you were going to make me take as a consort? If you thought she was capable of murder, perhaps you might have considered someone else for the role, mother." Radek retorted, struggling, and failing, to keep his anger out of his voice.

Genesa's brows raised to her hairline. "Tone, Radek. I may have erred when it came to Savta, but I'm still your liege and your mother."

"My apologies," Radek inclined his head, then

looked up with a start. "Wait. Did you just admit to making a mistake?"

"It has been known to happen." She sighed. "After you vanished, it was brought to my attention that I hadn't been entirely fair to you."

Piper joined the conversation. "Given that your son left the planet and risked your wrath and that of the temples because no one would believe him, I'd say that's a fair assessment."

His mother turned towards Piper. "I'd say your presence here is proof that the priests were wrong. You're truly one of us now?"

Radek stayed quiet. This was the moment his father had warned him would come, and Piper had asked him to let her handle it alone. She said she needed to prove herself to his mother. He wasn't sure that was necessary, but he had agreed, anyway.

"I am Romaki." Piper bared her teeth to show her fangs. "Humans don't have fangs, for one. We can't transform into dragons either, and magic is nothing more than a myth on my world." She held out a hand and whispered the words he'd taught her last night. A moment later she was holding a red rose. "Before I met your son, I didn't believe magic existed, and I certainly couldn't use it." She handed the rose to Radek, who used his magic to levitate the flower down the table and let it drift down to rest beside his mother's plate.

Genesa nodded. "I'm glad to see you still have your magic, Radek. Between this demonstration, and the appearance of both your dragons last night, the temples will be hard pressed to insist on further testing."

"The Gods haven't punished me."

One of Radek's brothers chimed in from further down the table. "It might have been easier if they had. Do you have any idea what will happen when news of this spreads?"

Radek glowered at his sibling. "Why do you all insist in treating me like I am a child? Of course, I know what will happen when this news spreads. The priests' hold over our citizens will loosen, there will be questions, followed by upheaval, fear, and then, hopefully, change. We are Romaki. We were a force to be reckoned with once, and by the Gods, I hope we will be again."

Several more of Radek's brothers and sisters started to speak, some of them agreeing while others were opposed.

After a minute or two, Genesa put a stop to the arguments. "Enough. I'm well aware of how each of you feels on this topic already. You've all come to me at various times to let me know your thoughts, but until now, I haven't shared mine with anyone but your father and Syna, who is my representative in the court of the Fire Dragon Clan. I have been aware for some time that there are factions among the temples who covet power and wealth above all else. They have been covertly manipulating my court and the court of our brethren in the south. Radek's announcement today will force them to take more direct action. We will have to counter those actions, but we will do so carefully. Open war with the temples will not benefit anyone. Am I clear?"

Radek nodded. Now he understood Syna and his father's veiled comments. Things *had* changed while he was away. Not only did his mother believe him, but she was ready to take action. This wasn't the way he had hoped change would come to his planet, but at least it would come.

They stayed locked away in that room for hours, discussing alternatives and making plans. For the first time in memory, his family was working together, letting go of their differences to find common ground. It wasn't easy, but no one gave up or walked out. Everyone was there because it was what needed to be done, not only to protect themselves but the people that looked to them for leadership.

It was a long, difficult day, and it was also one of the best days of his life. Through it all, Piper stayed at his side. She was his center, and she made it clear with every word she spoke, that she would support him, his family, and his people in the fight to come.

EPILOGUE

IT HAD BEEN a crazy year full of intrigue, family fights, power struggles, moments of crisis, and times of laughter and celebration. Now, Piper was heading to Pyros to see Aria for the first time since they'd said their goodbyes in the shuttle bay of the *Firebrand*. She couldn't wait to see her and Melody. The little sprout had grown into an adorable toddler, and in a few weeks, she'd have a new role as a big sister.

They were travelling aboard the first Romaki ship to be commissioned in more than a hundred years, built in one of Vadir's shipyards, the first of an entire fleet. The *Blue Horizon* was fast, beautiful, and represented everything she and Radek had been working towards since they'd returned to Romak.

Radek joined her as she stared at the only piece of art to grace the walls of their quarters. It was a painting of two blue and silver dragons flying through space with the Earth rising beneath them. It was a portrait

Lisa had created of her and Radek, flying back to the *Firebrand*. What made the painting even more special was the fact that Lisa had painted it months before Radek had even left Romak. It was the reason that Vadir had offered to take him with him that fateful day. Piper loved it.

"We'll be reducing speed in another hour or so. We're almost to the Pyrosian's home system."

"We made it here so fast Vadir will want to upgrade his engines again just so he can keep up with us."

"I suspect he already has. That male does not like to lose."

"He really doesn't."

Vadir had been one of their greatest allies over the past year, creating opportunities and introducing so many new technologies and goods that the Romaki had stopped fearing change and started to embrace it much faster than they had dared to hope. There were still years of work to be done to bring their world and its citizens back into step with the rest of the galaxy, but they were making progress, and that's all that mattered.

For now, though, their work on Romak was done. Radek had come into his own as a diplomat. He had brokered trade deals and established diplomacy with several races, including the Pyrosians and humans. To continue his work, his mother had sent them to Pyros to establish an embassy there. It was the first time any Romaki would live away from their homeworld in generations.

It wasn't the only embassy being established, either.

The Pyrosians were already on Earth, setting up a handful of locations across the globe where they would live and interact with humans. It had been Haley's idea. A way to help humanity adjust to the idea that they weren't alone in the universe and help them get to know the alien races on a more personal level. Haley's articles were helping too, and soon she'd be releasing her first book on what it was like to live on another planet. It was already a best seller.

The Star-Crossed Dating Agency was still operating, though now every female who applied knew exactly what they were agreeing to. Those with matches were quietly notified and transported to Pyros to meet their mates. There were no more Gatherings or high-profile events that might be targeted by the anti-alien groups. Like the Romaki, humanity would need time to adjust to the changes and learn to let go of their fear.

"What are you thinking about, *mila*?" Radek asked.

"I'm thinking about everything that's changed, and everything that hasn't." She leaned into his side and his arm slid around her waist. Her love for Radek was one of the things that hadn't changed. It had only grown deeper with the passing days.

"Change takes time. Not everyone is as fearless as you are."

"I know. I'm worried about the embassies on Earth, though. What if something happens and there are more injuries, or worse, more deaths?"

"The ones going are all volunteers. They know the risks. Besides, there will be Romaki at every location, and they have all sworn to protect and defend those embassies, and everyone in them." Radek chuckled. "As you know, we dragons are notoriously difficult to kill."

"True." There had been a few violent upheavals in some areas, mostly in places away from the capitals, where the priests held more influence over the populace than the rulers they were sworn to serve. She had witnessed the violence firsthand more than once and been stunned by the amount of damage the Romaki could take before they even showed signs of slowing.

"I just wish they'd caught the assholes who bombed the Gathering last year. If they were locked away, I'd worry less."

"Eventually they will all be caught. Once your species learns to accept their new allies, the ones who deal in fear and hate will have no place to hide."

"That's the same thing we've been saying about our fight on Romak."

He grinned at her. "Exactly."

"I'll try to be patient. Speaking of patience, how did your last chat with your mother go?" Things between Radek and the rest of his family had improved considerably since his return, but the habits of a lifetime weren't easy to unlearn, and his relationship with his mother still had adversarial moments.

"She still has concerns about sending our citizens to Earth, but she is willing to let the plan proceed. She said she trusts my judgement."

"No need to sound so surprised. If she didn't trust

you, we wouldn't be on our way to Pyros, and the *Blue Horizon* wouldn't exist."

"I know, but she actually said it out loud, to me."

She turned and looked up at her beloved mate. He still took her breath away, and she suspected he always would. "She loves you, and so do I."

"I know you do. I also know that you gave up your dream to help me fulfill mine. Now that we're moving on to a new adventure, I thought you might want to give your dream another shot."

"My dream? You mean to run a restaurant?" She started to bounce on her toes as her brain went into overdrive thinking of all the dishes she had learned to prepare since coming to Romak. "Where? When? How?"

"What better way to introduce people to our cultures than through food? I've spoken with Prince Joran, Aria, and Vadir, of course. They helped me design a restaurant that will operate as part of the embassy."

She squealed and threw her arms around his neck. "You did? Aria never said a word! Oh my god, I'm getting my own restaurant."

"You are. Aria says there are enough human females on Pyros now that there will be quite a demand for your services. Vadir is handling the import of all the necessary foods and equipment, and I believe he wants to talk to you about eventually expanding the idea to the embassies on Earth."

"Of course he does. And I think it's a great idea, but

I need to get the first one up and running." She kissed him happily. "Thank you."

"You're welcome, *sadina*." He lifted her higher and kissed her until her toes curled.

Elated, Piper was almost humming with joy as she kissed him back, her mind still awhirl with ideas for her new restaurant. She had everything she'd ever dreamed of, and so much more. She had a larger family, new friends, a purpose, and best of all, she had Radek. He was her rock. The one who brought love and magic into her life and filled her days with joy.

"Going to that Gathering was the best decision I ever made."

"Biting you was mine," he replied with a wink.

"I'm glad you feel that way because you know the rules. You bit me—"

He finished her sentence. "Now I'm stuck with you."

"Forever."

THE END

ABOUT THE INTERGALACTIC DATING AGENCY SERIES

Ready for more out of this world romances? The adventure isn't over yet! Fly over to our dating agency website to check out more stories from this multi-author series. The Intergalactic Dating Agency is ready and waiting to set you up with a host of alien hotties from all over the galaxy.

Make a date with your alien match today.

http://romancingthealien.com

Want to read more stories with book boyfriends that are out of this world?

Check out Susan Hayes' other Science Fiction Romance Titles

The Drift
Double Down
All In
Wild Card
Three of a Kind
No Limit
Blind Bet
Aces Over Queen

Nova Force
Operation Phoenix
Operation Cobalt

3013: The Series
3013: RENEGADE
3013: STOWAWAY
3013: TARGETED
3013: FATED
3013: SCARRED

www.ingramcontent.com/pod-product-compliance
Lightning Source LLC
Chambersburg PA
CBHW021729190726
48288CB00009B/2972